THE WILDERNESS

WITHIN

By
John Claude Smith

Trepidatio Publishing

TREPIDATIO
PUBLISHING

Trepidatio books may be ordered through booksellers or by contacting:

Trepidatio Publishing an imprint of JournalStone

www.trepidatio.com

The views expressed in this work are solely those of the authors and do not necessarily reflect the views of the publisher, and the publisher hereby disclaims any responsibility for them.

ISBN: 978-1-945373-93-0   (sc)
ISBN: 978-1-945373-94-7   (ebook)

JournalStone rev. date: October 6, 2017

Library of Congress Control Number: 2017948074

Printed in the United States of America
1st JournalStone Edition

Cover Art & Design: Kerry Ellis/99designs
Hand photo: © Xmee
Branches: © Angeles Balaguer
Edited by: Aaron J. French

For my wonderful friend and co-conspirator in the exploration of "Zen entertainment," Fred Shaw.

ACKNOWLEDGMENTS

Big thanks to my publishers Jess Landry and Christopher C. Payne of Trepidatio/JournalStone, and to Aaron J. French (and astute proofreader, Sean Leonard), whose keen editorial assistance helped shape the novel in your hands.

Thanks to the early readers of the novel, whose invaluable feedback helped me wrap my head around the tale: Heath Yonaites, Alessandra Bava, Sabine Hope, and especially my mad "sister," Sharene Martin-Brown.

Thank you, dear readers (and fellow writers), for the support. I appreciate the time you take to spend with the tales I weave from my dark corner of the weird universe.

THE WILDERNESS

WITHIN

Outside

"I believe it possible for our consciousness to change and grow, and that with this change we may become aware of a new universe."
—Algernon Blackwood

"I am not sure that I exist, actually. I am all the writers that I have read, all the people that I have met, all the women that I have loved; all the cities I have visited."
—Jorge Luis Borges

"It is sometimes an appropriate response to reality to go insane."
—Philip K. Dick

Prelude: Ouroboros I

It wasn't the wind that awakened me. I'd grown accustomed to its mysterious habits, the fluid rhythms of its rhyme and reason. It came in waves, surging up to the shore of my house, whistling along the wooden walls and jangling the windowpanes. It would rattle about, only to recede into the emptiness from whence it came. Not like this other sound. This other sound awakened me, lingering in the air, clearing out the mist of mental debris and already forgotten dreams. Here I am, ready or not.

I'd been patient. I was ready.

This other sound buzzed and crackled and breathed deep as the fathomless space between me and out there—

The forest.

Six months waiting, patient, and finally, something of substance.

I'd read in the newspapers and had done much internet research, gleaning the basics of what had transpired in this forest four years ago, while I'd spent a year on sabbatical in a cottage outside of Wales, much as Robert Plant and Jimmy Page had done for a few months at Bron-Yr-Aur prior to recording the third Led Zeppelin LP. Soaking up the ambience and refreshing my soul in the pursuit of my art.

While away, the forest, and this house at the edge of the forest, were never far from my thoughts.

What had kept me away had less to do with the facts, and more to do with the rumors.

And visions.

Perhaps through seeing in a different light, one whittled to clarity by the passage of time, and with different eyes, sense would be made of the onslaught of visions that took over my mind.

The sounds lift my spirit on parchment wings into the gloaming, but

I have no fear of falling. I raise a quartz crystal to my right eye, altering the landscape. Something primordial scurries at the edge, something I sense has always been here. The mix of familiar and obscure tones enthralls me as my spirit is lifted ever higher—

And I see him…

1: The Godfather of Goth

"Goddamn, that's beautiful," I said, smiling at Frank as shadows did a herky-jerky dance across his forlorn countenance.

The sky above Frank and me was impossibly vast, bloated with stars, unveiling secrets and seductions that only these circumstances could inspire. Out here at Frank's place, edge of the woods, a pit fire roaring in front of us, but I barely noticed it, only felt its heat.

A coyote bayed in the distance, somewhere just beyond Frank's log cabin castle. The coyote's solitary wail soared across the heavens and slithered into the deeper darkness between the stars. Hundreds, thousands of eyes staring back at us, as if watching.

Despite the pit fire, a chill skipped like a stone across the calm waters of my spine.

"It's beautiful, but it's dangerous, Derek," Frank said, after thirty seconds of verbal silence, as if mesmerized by the coyote's midnight serenade or possibly the snap, crackle, and pop of the logs, twigs, and splintered hardback chair being devoured by flames.

Frank Harlan Marshall, always the somber philosopher, always bathed in black. The Godfather of Goth, I called him, a reference to his dark side fascinations and moods. More for my amusement as he hasn't a clue or interest in "Goth" culture and doesn't utilize gothic trappings in his fiction.

"How so?"

He shrugged his shoulders, tilted his head, searching. Turning to me, he mouthed something that was muffled by another coyote's wail.

"What?" I asked, pointing to my ear, shaking my head: *no comprende.*

He shook his head as well, and the look made me uncomfortable.

I'd known Frank for thirty years, ever since we were mischievous kids growing up in Tucson, Arizona, plotting our escape from the tarantulas, tumbleweeds, and summer storms that were forgotten twenty minutes after they'd passed. The humidity ate our souls, while the desire for something more fueled our spirits, even at the tender age of ten.

Tender, but not innocent. Never innocent.

We read voraciously, both of us driven by words, by the descriptive fantasies, captivating realities, detailed deviances, and capricious promises that the world beyond this parched, dust-laden landscape was the world we wanted to experience.

We started writing at an early age, spent the passing time with pens and pads of paper and scavenged word processors. Scraps of inspiration and fanciful interludes that relieved us of the drudgery of the serenity that was our lives. That filled the days until college took us to California and the novels started pouring out, and the serenity we so wanted to escape from became a new dream, but not one we spoke of openly.

The ride was too damned fun.

We'd been through marriages, girlfriends, rehab (and marriage- and girlfriend-inspired rehab), all while the writing endeavors led us to "best seller" status and the lifestyle hijinks that inspired much of our writing, though I certainly hoped the core of his writing—horror of the grimmest sort—had nothing to do with any personal lifestyle hijinks I was not privy to. That said there were no secrets between us, and yet his current harried, exhausted look worried me.

He pulled a joint from the inside pocket of his denim jacket and rolled it between his thumb and fingers. Iron Maiden, Megadeth, Metallica and more were embroidered all over the blue fabric canvas, shoulder to waist, no space wasted amidst heavy metal clutter. Christ, a joint. I hadn't partaken in the ingestion of drugs of any sort, besides over-the-counter medication to blot out headaches or stomach ailments, in many years. My body didn't enjoy it anymore.

"For old times' sake, Cisco," he said. The use of the goofball nickname seemed out of place; then again, maybe this was a good sign. He lit up and took a deep drag, seeming to suck in whatever was bothering him with the motion. His eyelids fluttered and shut as he welcomed the smoke. The tip of the joint grew bright as neon.

I decided to play along. What the hell—that's what friends were for. Maybe this would open him up and let me in, as if that had ever been a problem before. But this visit had come at his request, out of the blue. We saw each other fairly often, but this one seemed tinged with something more, an email missive: "Cisco, there's much to show you. Much that you might find intriguing. Come now, please. Pancho."

Strange: a terse request, that's all. Not like his usual sarcastic worldview volleys and rambling asides, this one was to the point. Which was never Frank's way. Since I had gotten here earlier in the day he had been cordial but not forthcoming, which was not what I expected from him, too close to the clipped tone of the email.

Something was definitely amiss.

I took the joint and sucked hard. The smoke burned, bristled at my throat, caught there and begged escape. I held on until the cough demanded release, a hard bark that scratched as claws at my singed tonsils. A sudden rush flushed all cohesive thought from my head and pasted a sneaky smile across my face.

"I haven't done that since Izzy's party."

"You didn't even take a hit there, remember…?"

I thought hard and laughed. Contact high. Frank was right. Amidst the private party for our good friend, comedian extraordinaire, Isadora "Dizzy Izzy" Haberstein, the makeshift performance stage at the closed down club, Radiance, was hot with the burnt sweet-into-pungent smells of the seductive smoke. Izzy's birthday stand-up performance was something to behold, something he hadn't done in years, since his own success had taken him to higher plateaus, full of classic crude humor and humorous asides, some of us knowing we were the inspiration. Izzy was on fire, that room was a furnace, burning at my eyes, my head. I puked upon leaving, thankfully not in full view of the rest of the guests and later, a couple months at most, Izzy left a message of a spontaneous marriage to a woman he had introduced us to at the performance, and that was the last we'd heard from him.

From stand-up to HBO sitcom smash hit, as well as a trio of blockbuster movies, he still found time to privately entertain those who really mattered to him, like at that birthday party.

But afterwards, it was as if he had fallen off the edge of the earth.

Frank put out his hand, fingers twitching a jittery two-step like those tarantulas from so long ago. I passed the joint to him and he smiled. But the smile was still scarred with something deeper. His mind seemed full of something that my stay would pull out. At least I hoped.

He'd made his initial impact with the Average Joe series, taut, graphic exercises in cat and mouse deception, starring his fractured genius, Detective Bob, and the lone blemish on his record, the enigmatic serial killer, Average Joe. A trilogy of hit movies based on the series embedded him in the public consciousness.

Needing a change, to shake up expectations, he killed off Average Joe in a forest, an execution carried out by the unseen forces of nature—a place saturated with evil—and birthed his follow-up Sinister Nature series. (And "killed" might be too strong a word: Frank never clarified the circumstances of Average Joe's strange disappearance...) Though a distinctive antagonist such as Average Joe was never given face, the breadth of supernatural menace appealed on a broader scope than even Frank had imagined possible, triggering a string of N.Y. Times number one bestsellers and two hit movies, so far.

Under the circumstances, I found his moving out here to the edge of the forest a year ago rather surprising, as if he was giving in to his own demons. I wondered if he was testing himself, or if the move had been prompted by a desire for hands-on research, or if there was some other elusive explanation. Though we had no secrets, it's not as if we knew everything there was to know about each other. I'm sure there's stuff in Frank's head that would disgust me, what with the focus of his fiction. Either way, I found it surprising, and not in a good way.

I watched him stare into the pit fire, as best his delinquent pupils would allow, the flames now viciously snapping at the sky. Ragged edges born from smooth, fluid origins, when the fire was young and cautious. Now it fought for a place amongst the empty spaces. Now it seemed to vibrate, to resonate, with life, with purpose.

The sky looked uncomfortably crowded and not pleased with the intrusion.

Frank turned to me and said, "I need to show you something, Derek. I need to show you something..."

2: Comic Relief

The wooden house was cold. The planks and logs supplied shelter, but the lack of substantial insulation meant the weather outside sternly dictated the temperature inside. Hence, if it was cold outside, you were rarely warm enough inside; if it was hot outside, you baked. None of the drizzly rain I got in San Francisco, where I lived. When it rained here, I'm sure it was of a proportion Noah would appreciate.

Earlier we had spent a couple hours chopping wood, me enjoying the brute physicality of swinging an axe and having it dig deep into a log. A hydraulic wood-splitter actually did most of the work, no matter my testosterone-fueled efforts. But even there, it was necessary for us to muscle a tree stump onto the gas powered machine and pull the lever. The hydraulic force shoved the blade into the stump and ripped it to the core. I might have to bang away with the blunt side of the axe head to knock it apart, but the exercise was, at least for me, welcome. I looked at it as a workout, always struggling to stay fit.

Not like Frank. He'd let himself go and has had a couple recent stints of alcoholism that hinted at derailing his career, only to step out of rehab with the inspiration for the next hit novels. Hell, I'd done that a couple times early in my career, but realized that my brain did not like functioning in recovery mode all the time, so I cut back to the extreme on the drug and alcohol vices, with my own major blips along the way.

We were an odd yin and yang, our differences balancing us, but not so much as to not overlap at some points. We had fun together and had fun always, usually triggered by one of our triumvirate of weakness: loud music, travel, and women. Our excesses, despite my current aspirations for health, were always indulgent to the point of ridiculous. Only over the last five years have I actually gotten hold of my excesses, taking up the health regime. But not so much as to deter the fun to be had when we were together. I just paid for it the few days afterward, recuperating, staying in bed and reading too much. So be it. We were a strange mix, but good friends.

The yin and yang became more apparent when I took in the concentrated chaos that was his décor. I would play Felix to his Oscar, my condo pristine, well, not quite pristine (and me not quite Felix), but more a concentrated dishevelment. But at least there was sense to be made of the mess. The litter of his history, and much of our history, haphazardly filled the confines of the front room. Awards, photos, and books crammed in overstuffed bookshelves, strewn across table tops, precariously balanced on top of the television. Frank had always been a slob. It just seemed messier in this wooden house. I glanced around and spotted the handful of Bram Stoker awards scattered about the room, two of them toppled, buried under the dust which coated everything here, and a lone Shirley Jackson award. There were statues and framed certificates from our youth, of this or that writing contest he had won, and even the ugly puce ribbons we had both won when we were eleven and tied for first place in a creative writing contest. I had to shake my head and smile, Frank's nostalgia worthy of at least that much.

We threw huge slabs of wood into the wood stove, the name chiseled into the metal front incomplete—Bradf-*something*—barely legible, not a uniform fading. As I recalled, Bradford was a famous wood stove manufacturer. If this was any indication of their workmanship, the quality had deteriorated severely, but in a way that made it seem more as if a pen had run out of ink as one was writing, which hit me as anomalous: the whole house seemed to be in perpetual flux, unfinished, awaiting something or at least something *more*. The wood stove feebly attempted to heat the whole place. We sat in front of it, feet propped on the bricks below it, warming our soles and souls.

Frank pulled out a crumpled letter and handed it to me.

"You get mail up here?" I smiled. He pointed at the return address, the name.

"Christ, Izzy?"

"Yeah, that's part of the reason I brought out the smoke. Jogging your memory."

"I remember that night and the woman he introduced to us, Jessie something, long dark hair like a waterfall of ink, eyes radiant and unreal."

"Right. She was, well, without meaning to sound rude, she was out of his league, or...no" — the look in his eyes suggested a rearranging of perceptions — "they were of different leagues. Izzy was so out of it he was in a league of his own."

So true, I thought.

I flipped up the already unsealed flap and pulled out the single sheet of paper. I read the childlike printing. The printing made me uncomfortable. The message didn't alleviate this feeling.

frank
did i ever tell you the one about the writer who...
ive seen things and know things
will be by early oct
isadora

"The writer who — what?" I said, trying to read between the lines, no X marked treasures to be found. It was vague at best, perplexing for sure. The line, "Did I ever tell you the one about..." had been Izzy's hook since the beginning of his stand-up career, milked to overuse in the movies and on his hit HBO sitcom, *Psychobabble,* in which he played a celebrity psychoanalyst who is more neurotic than his patients. It was a trademark, much as Jeff Foxworthy's "You might be a redneck" riff was indelibly linked to him.

Having known Izzy for seven years prior to his disappearance and just wishing the best for him since, this didn't sound like him at all. It sounded mysterious and Izzy was always blunt, graphic, in your face. And signing it "isadora," this was inconceivable. He once told me never to call him Isadora, "Under threat of eternal unga bunga at the hands of an insatiable tribe of homosexual natives"—unga bunga being the tribal equivalent of sodomy in a joke he used to tell about a choice between death and unga bunga, the first captive choosing unga bunga, only to be gang raped by the whole tribe, while the second captive, not wanting the two days' onslaught, chose death instead, only to have death be by unga bunga, of course. Frank and I found this sophomoric humor at the hands of Izzy disgusting, yet quite funny, because we knew him, but also because he was an outlandish performer, bent over and moaning like a constipated elephant. He reminded me of the first time I'd seen Jim Carrey in *Ace Ventura*, talking ass and all, and the *idiocy* of it all, yet laughing at the crude bravado. Where *Ace Ventura* was distracting one time and infantile thereafter, I'd heard Izzy's joke dozens of times during stand-up performances early in his career and it never ceased to nail the audience and me to the wall, hanging next to wooden spoons and misplaced donkey tails.

Back to the letter, I found his signature, not even a capitol "I," the most disturbing element of all.

I shook my head and looked at Frank.

"I got that a few weeks ago. That's why I wanted you here. I'm not in the best shape to deal with the reappearance of Dizzy Izzy, at least not in the state of mind that letter portends. If he sounded like himself, I'd have invited you anyway, for a long week or three of madness. But this seems..."

He trailed off, the sentence incomplete. Just like the surroundings, I thought.

"What else, Frank? You seem...well, there's something more, right?"

"Yeah, been writing forever, long as I've known you. Been a constant thing, no hassles, no stopping, everything torn from the brain and set down on paper, even when some thought I had hit the wall." He snickered. "And even when some hoped I had hit the wall, life and all in turmoil. But recently, since about the time of the letter, well, I'm in the middle of a novel. I've really hit the wall— face first, no forgiveness, no nothing. That's a first."

"A writer's block?" I snorted, not that it was funny, more at my surprise. Frank was a good writer, but more nuts-and-bolts than artistically driven. He had sequences where his mastery of words detailed something of scintillating beauty, as well as moments where supreme ugliness prevailed—one of his strengths—where it all gelled and became something more, but for the most part, he was a machine. A profitable, well-oiled machine.

"I thought you'd never get to experience the confidence-jarring joy of a writer's block. But you know you'll pull through. I have the two times it hit me hard."

My writer's blocks had been at the end of both of my marriages. Stress I assumed. Getting past the pain of one and chaos of the other, the writing exploded and two novels followed, both completed in less than three months of white hot, white knuckle intensity. But that was after six months in one case and nine in the other. Writing nothing of worth. Stumbling, confidence deflated. Nothing.

Afterwards, since I wrote about the human condition, more so-called "literary" than Frank's work, yet still with a fantastical edge—occasional reviews hitched me along the same lines as Katrina Santinia and Lucius Sheppard (I never saw it), or Mikael Toivonen, whose surreal take on magic realism was the closest to mine, but still quite different—I figured the writer's blocks were me processing the hell out of it all and finally picking, or having my brain pick, the appropriate path and laying it all out. A healing catharsis.

"Don't worry about it. You'll probably write the best work of your life when it passes."

"I don't think so. Something's off in ways I can't explain. I've been doing this horror gig for a long time, and now it seems to be seeping into my life." A quick jerk of the head, a dim smile at his lips. "There've been a lot of unexplained incidents, observations, perceptions—what-have-you—over the last couple months, writing the novel, that have left me wondering."

"Wondering about what? You're a good writer. You know it will come back to you sooner than later. I mean, there're times I wish I had your ability to just grind through when things were tough. Maybe it's just time to grind through until something kicks in and feels right again. Like you've always done in the face of adversity."

"Nah, it's *different* than that. I know I can write. I wonder about madness. Reality. I feel as if all my horrors are creeping in to take over. Haunting me." He paused, staring at the wall, a thousand-yard stare that threatened to burn through and reach out to the forest, setting it ablaze. "The letter from Izzy is confirmation in some strange way that everything is off."

"Well, yeah, a letter from a person you haven't heard from in almost eight years, odd for sure, but not so odd." I shrugged my shoulders. "Probably just as weird it was a letter and not an email. But he was your friend. He was *our* friend. These things happen. But it seems you're blowing it all out of proportion. Maybe you're just exhausted and need a break and this is the way your brain is telling you to take one. That said"—me, prying as I am wont to do, jumping back to something that elbowed my interest a couple minutes earlier—"what unexplained incidents have transpired?"

"Just stuff. Izzy is the capper, but…"

"C'mon, Frank. Ever since I got here you've been…you *haven't* been yourself. You've been evasive and that's just not your way. You've always been an open book with me, which I don't mean as an insult or anything negative. I've been as open or more with you as well. You know this. So what's up? What incidents?"

Frank hesitated, looked around at everything, and, really, at nothing. His mind was wandering; his eyes were following.

"You stay here a bit, you'll see."

Even though we saw each other frequently, I'd only been here once before and that as a stop off, picking him up as we headed to an airport, and England. I thought it beautiful, but there was always a mystery, or perhaps an intangible degree of danger, to nature that tainted the beauty.

Frank got up and headed toward the bathroom. I would have persisted, but he seemed determined not to follow up with anything more than unfocused eyes and convoluted headshakes, as if too much was traipsing within his skull, looking for a way out.

I guess it would take time.

This was a first. Frank Harlan Marshall was hands down the most prolific horror writer of the last fifteen years; well, him and some guy named King, who'd been doing it as long as we'd been alive. Explaining the unexplainable was Frank's forte. Though he was very much a machine, showing the true face of evil and dread was his specialty. He thrived on enveloping the reader in the graphic grotesqueries, to discomfiting effect. His fan base thrived on this vicarious connection.

I felt it was going to be a long week or three here, at least. I wondered if Frank would come around and sound like himself, and if Izzy would show up and seem like himself after all these years, and…what was that sound from next door?

3: Dark Angel Asylum

"She's a musician, a vocalist, used to sing for some industrial metal conglomerate, like Pigface but not Pigface. Early nineties tattered edge of technology put to sounds. I think she does some solo work now, the occasional CD. She must be practicing for something, though, what with…"

Frank canted his head toward the caterwauling sounds from next door; next door not exactly "next" door, but the closest neighbor to one side. There was plenty of space between houses.

The caterwauling sounds seemed strangely familiar.

"Nineties industrial metal—who?"

"Not sure." He took a shot at it, thinking out loud. "Angel Dark…insane…something…"

"Oh, Christ, Dark Angel Asylum? Dark Angel Asylum?"

"I think that's it." He grinned, a sly, deceptive, foxlike leer, as if playing a game of which only he knew the rules.

"Alethea?"

"Yeah, that's her name, Alethea. Never met her, just know it's her through gossip by the locals in town."

I'd discovered Dark Angel Asylum over the last few years, one of those bands that, once having discovered, means so much to a person. How I'd missed them while they were together was beyond me. How we'd missed them with all of the concerts we had gone to really miffed me as they fit into so much that I liked about music, creativity, the outsider mindset within the world: creating because you had to, not because you fit into something that was currently popular. Dark Angel Asylum only got dumped into the industrial metal classification because they veered that way, not because that was really what they were doing. It's not as if they fit into any particular style. They'd been most often categorized as the aforementioned industrial metal and even gothic. The more astute journalists saw a relation to the late 70s, early 80s no wave movement that was popular in New York. I thought this a valid observation. There was even a minute where some feeble-minded publicist or greedy label head honcho attempted to broaden popularity by designating Dark Angel Asylum as an offshoot of grunge, a curse bestowed on many bands during the early 90s. They had zero to do with grunge.

The band was originated by Aleister Blut, a force of nature vocalist, guitarist and lyricist, who wrote songs about societal dehumanization in a world of crass commercialism, the corruption of the masses and the world itself in the land of the free and the home of the oppressed. A message more potent in the current age. Alethea had joined after the first release, the harsh dynamics of that record redefining heavy electronic music, not unlike Raptor Elegance, but still wholly their own breed of audio animal.

With her assimilation into the band, the tones changed as the music shifted into a more varied aural landscape. The fourth release, 1997's *The Adoration of Decay*, is generally considered the peak of their career, a defining moment in dark, loud music, their heaviest release since the first one. They released one more disc, 2001's *Dreaming of Now*, a primarily ambient exercise, sparse lyrics, samples pulled from the world around them, kind of a postcard on the decline of the human race near the end of the millennium.

The band split up amidst a turbulent world tour that same year, in which Aleister Blut disappeared, only to resurface six months later living a "normal" life in a white stucco house in Phoenix, Arizona. Six months after that he disappeared again, only to end up in a mental institute a few months later. At this point the story becomes sketchy, the reasons and circumstances of his stay never clarified.

He has spent all of his time since then in the mental institute. Occasional reports on his condition are featured on the entertainment news shows, often including photos snapped from outside the institute's walls. He always looked frail and generally decrepit in ways that were more than disturbing.

That was part of my interest in the band; after having seen one of these reports, I wanted to know more about them. Aleister Blut's strange existence post-Dark Angel Asylum had prodded my interest, but Alethea's unique presence shifted my interest to her and her music, then and now.

I read everything I could about her, from biographic profiles to oblique interviews that raised more questions than they answered.

Alethea had lived on the streets of New York for a year—"a sociological experiment, not life at a glance, but immersed in it, the living"—before creating the all-female psychopunk/noise band, Slot Junky. She split that up when she heard of the tumultuous state of affairs within the borders of Dark Angel Asylum, Blut's dissatisfaction with the first incarnation's members "turning into rock stars, when that's not what we're about, not what I'm about. I'm here to make a fucking point about this pitiful planet and we humans who corrupt it with our mere existence." She ignored rumors of Blut's volatility, joining the band during a massive restructuring of forces to fit Blut's ideals. Ideals which she found appealing and essential as well. Her understanding of his focus for the band eased her into the passenger seat for a ride that was wild, explorative, and revelatory. But much to Blut's chagrin, her growth did not stop at his singular, bone-polishing obsessions. She appreciated his ideals, but was forever expanding on them with her own contributions.

Since the break-up she has released three CDs, fascinating excursions into her own psychosis, both the good and the bad, the dark and the light, the mixture of positive and negative a balance that her outsider mindset "never viewed as anything less than necessary." With the proper direction, she could be popular in the same way P.J. Harvey was popular, kind of an artist on her own exploring all *her* obsessions. The stark, myriad mental obsessions, as well as the unsettled musical territories they required for presentation. But where Harvey's skills at pop song structures were always evident, Alethea occasionally dabbled without fully diving in: she was into something *different*. She had a huge club hit in 2005 with "Kosmic Kiss," but the CD it was taken from, *Foreign/Alien*, was a schizophrenic tour de force of paranoia and self-analysis—more balance there, observations from the inside as well as the outside, looking in—her vocals sometimes beautiful, as with the hit, while at other times she was a demon (succubus incarnate), a child, an old woman, the ageless essence of self from beyond birth, past lives, or whatever was necessary within the constructs of the atypical transmissions of the music.

I found these excursions most impressive in their unrelenting exploration of the depths of herself, her heart, her being. I'd actually based a peripheral character in my most recent novel, *Blank Postcard*, on her, the luminous, mysterious Ashlyn Cage. A peripheral character I wanted to bring more into view in the next novel.

I'd had many conversations about this with Frank, to the point where he called me obsessive. This also made his coy, dumb guy response to who lived next door rather peculiar. If he'd have let on that Alethea, the inspiration in the flesh, lived next door, I'm sure I would have been back up here months ago, and maybe we could have averted whatever was in motion now.

I nodded to the unearthly sounds—a voice, yes, but a voice used in a way no human has ever used a voice before—tempted to go over and introduce myself, but I also knew the creative mindset and if she was locked in, an interruption would not be welcome.

It seemed her voice overrode everything as the wailing coyotes fell silent, as if they were contemplating what strange animal was making these fierce, feral sounds.

I knew I wanted to get to know the animal much better, even if it was for no other reason than my own selfish conceits, fleshing out a character and adding color to a charcoal drawing.

4: Gone Fishing

"Let's take a walk, Cisco."

Frank's voice cut through the sleep haze, each word pummeling as a boulder would drop through the funneled waist of a humungous hourglass upon my head.

Wake up!

"What time is it?" I said, the words shifting tectonically, as if the boulder had been crushed into bite-sized rocks and my mouth was stuffed to the gills and more, my tongue paralyzed by the interruption in my sleep, for which I should have been thankful, what with the warped subject matter infiltrating my dreams.

Sleep was only partially attained, most of the night spent in battle with the demons and memories that decided to ambush any allusions toward rest with clipped, flashpoint images, or worse. Twisting and slinking through a labyrinthine Boschian landscape: a seething nightmare that devoured any rest rooted in the foundation of reality. Frank's voice triggered the nightmare world to release me, puke me into awareness, too early or, at least, before it was done with me. I was cognizant of Frank's miasmal mood the previous evening and wondered if that was the inspiration for my disturbing dreams, and of a wood stove that never lifted the chill from my bones. I'm sure I looked like death, not warmed over, but sinking into the dismal depths of dead-eyed and darker socket inspired weariness.

The night seemed so very long.

The dreams sprawled, crisscrossed over each other, octopus' tentacles thrashing without intent, unable to latch onto any single image, the many images morphing into each other: a catacomb pulsing as a heart; tiny, illegible graffiti stitched with catgut across my naked skull; sap spilling like blood from axe-wounded tree stumps. And more surreptitiously, memories of people I had known, only perverted as everything else: my ex-wife (number one), Doreen, smiling, but the smile seemed decayed, teeth like termite riddled wood, undefined things, but *not* termites, squirming in the knots; my ex-wife (number two), Asia, laughing, but the sound was like rust and shaved metal passing through a sieve, amplified, crying, wheezing. Moments of failure that required no enhancement. Moments of success rimmed with something unhealthy. Moments, like reflections in a broken mirror, each shard another moment, a cracked chain-link connection between events years apart.

Borges' epigram on mirrors tossed on its side—"mirrors and copulation are abominable, for they multiply the numbers of mankind"—as delineated by the savage folly of dream logic in fearless, Full Monty display.

It seemed the past had come to poke a sharp stick at the gray matter pin cushion of my thoughts. I only hoped this was the last of it.

"Cisco, get up," Frank said, more a coo than a bark, as if this subtler mode of attack would matter.

"What goddamn time is it?"

My eyelids hesitantly opened, as if the chain within the tear ducts was being hand-cranked without real inspiration, only to reveal Frank's leering face too close to mine, a monstrosity of humongous proportions: Shrek, about to kiss the bride.

"What the fuck, I'm up," I said, throwing the tattered, red and green plaid blanket to the floor. Frank did not flinch, so I knew he was still in his mood. Usually this kind of thing makes me testy. Frank knows waking me up early or at least before I am ready to be awakened is borderline suicidal, a deathwish I'm quite willing to fulfill.

"What's the hurry?" I ran my hand through my hair, the tousled black mass rearranged into a lopsided pompadour, a hirsute leaning tower of Pisa.

"Take a walk with me," he said, fishing pole and tackle box in tow. Early morning fishing jaunts did not rate high on my "to do" list, but I figured since I was here and Frank was in a mood, might as well go. It might chip through his so far murky disposition.

I slipped into some grey cargo pants and a threadbare Qod Torren T-shirt, remnant of our early 2000s predilection toward everything electro-industrial. I was ripe for something: coffee? A fight?

But I had to jump to it to catch up with Frank as he was already headed out the back door. Socks were deemed unnecessary; the red Converse sneakers would have to do.

"What's the hurry?"

"No hurry, it's just..." Fading like sun-scattered mist, this thought.

No, we were not going to do this again. Well, not on this level.

"No more games, it's just what?"

Frank glanced my way, could read that I was not in the mood to pussyfoot about. Still, that did not mean he would be revealing anything of substance, but he knew me in the morning. No messing about. Get to it!

"Remember that trip we took to Auschwitz?"

Okay, where did this come from?

"How could I forget it," I said, my memories drifting back in time, sifting through debris, impressions.

"Remember how I just wanted to soak in it, to know it, to sense what had transpired there, looking for something, for somewhere else to take the fiction?"

The trip was an offshoot of one of our European vacations, a side-step, Frank having seen a photo exhibit in a dingy, off the beaten path art gallery on the outskirts of Scotland. The photos depicted Auschwitz, "Then and Now," and Frank was visibly shaken by how the more current photos—dead chimneys all lined in a row; the bleak, soul-beaten landscape surrounding them—carried an ambience that, as he'd put it, "disallowed anything of worth ever to be constructed there. I'd thought they were reminders, but being here, seeing it and sensing it, the depth of the evil or maybe, more so, the raw, unrestrained influence or at least interaction of *the nature of this place,* there is no cleansing of what happened here. It's good that a fancy restaurant or a generic strip mall hasn't been constructed here, because there's evidence that this place, *the place itself,* would always be imbued with its own darkly persuasive *personality,* in some form, somehow."

I remember sensing that weight as well, though not as extreme as Frank. Still, I couldn't wait to leave. I also figured that Frank's mindset, more fascinated by true darkness, was eager to embrace something of this nature. I was sure he would take something there and utilize it in his fiction.

When we got back to the states, Frank had found a couple images online that worked for this mindset: a black and white perspective shot of the chimneys and an unrelated shot that featured the blackened husks of dead trees, victims of a forest fire. His next novel, *Black Eden,* was the linking novel between the Average Joe series and his new Sinister Nature series.

I have always found it profoundly disturbing, his most potent piece of work, but not one I go to when I want to reacquaint myself with something he has written.

"I remember a lot about that place. Bad place."

"Exactly. Bad place. You sensed it as well, I know."

"I know, I did. So what's your point?"

We had stepped into the forest beyond the dried out dirt and weeds, brambles in abundance. I hadn't even noticed how deep we'd gone into the forest, only now rubbing the sleep from my eyes, paying attention to Frank and not our path.

The cold had also lifted, as if it had never actually visited. It was muggy, not quite hot, but leaning that way.

"I believe that places incorporate the impressions that have been left on them. Evil or pain—"

"Or joy, happiness. Why does it have to be negative?"

"Well, sure, something positive, sure"—as if he really felt as though something positive was an option—"but evil or negativity seems more in sync with the essentiality of nature, with the nature of nature," he said, through a grim, tight-lipped smile.

"You're losing me…"

"I think in some cases these places, having grown accustomed to those impressions, might find themselves in need of them, of what has been extracted. Somehow. Through paranormal or supernatural means. They might even subtly persuade the minds of those who pass within their undefined range of influence. Maybe to fill the need again, of what has been missing."

"You're reaching, Pancho. I mean, we're all allotted free will, so what makes you think a place that's had something good or bad transpire within its borders can actually impose something, some kind of force or influence, as you say, on an individual?"

"If I said there was evidence you'd want examples of which…" At least he seemed to understand that my patience already was wearing tissue thin and tearing at the edges. "Maybe what I'm trying to say is that some places can amplify the good or bad within an individual and feed off it."

"Sounds like a great idea for a horror story." I felt he was trying to work through something, but this was a similar conversation to the ones we'd had after he had completed *Black Eden*, and all I really remember was that we took a trip to Venice soon thereafter and the impressions there—Italian women (my most prevalent weakness) and too much vino—were wondrous on many levels.

He stopped walking. I almost bumped into him, looped around and faced him. His attention was elsewhere, taking in the trees—blue pines, ponderosa pines, maybe some cedars—and the patchy gray sky beyond the tips of the trees. He peered into the distance, as if aware of something more that he could not bring into focus. Again, the thousand-yard stare.

"What's going on, my friend?" I did not like what I sensed here, with him.

Or so I thought it was "with him," this intangible "what" that I sensed.

"Don't you feel it here?" Wrinkles laced as confused, cursive script across his forehead, his eyelids scrunched, the light within his eyes quivering, almost pleading for me to understand.

"Sense what?" I said, fooling neither of us.

I sensed *something*, a discomfort that was like the weight of everything I had felt at Auschwitz, or at least a similar, immeasurable mass. I sensed an undefined something here as I stopped looking to Frank for answers, burrowing into my own mind for perceptions rooted in a consciousness I understood, to try and make sense of the ambience that even in this empty space seemed to crowd into me. The claustrophobic embrace of nothingness, but nothingness with presence.

The forest before this spot was perfunctory. Since I hadn't been paying attention the images I could pull up of the last twenty minutes' walk to this point were vague at best. They were images that fit into the catalogue my brain has of forests. There was nothing distinctive because my brain was looking inward, not all around me.

Until now.

Taking in the forest here, I scanned the whole of where I was and everything that surrounded me. The trees were maybe ten yards in a loose circumference from where we were standing. The glade was threaded with a carpet of branches, twigs, weeds, and mushrooms, thicker than outside of the circle, from what I could see. A handful of tree stumps jutted forth, having been witness— been participants—to some kind of violence. Probably something natural in nature, yet the trees that had been connected to the torn stumps were nowhere to be found. The stumps were covered in a bruised yellow into black moss that looked more like disease than anything of florid health. Gray lichen covered the larger rocks that dotted the glade.

Spider webs stretched across the expanse, a lattice whose prominence made my skin itch. I could not imagine how many spiders it had taken to create this death net hotel, yet further investigation showed no trespassing insects were cocooned within. The hotel seemed dead itself, the vacancy, permanent.

The smell of the place didn't deter my rising discomfort. The omnipresent earthy odors were cut with a stench that seemed of animal origin. Not musky, though something similar, rich and tangy. Injury bandaged with moss, never healing, always moist, the moss thriving on that which seeped from within.

The trees at the rim of our circle were tinted with the odd moss as well, as if the disease that had stricken the stumps had spread beyond, to feed on the more vital trees.

Beyond what I saw and smelled, I had a sense that something

was quite simply *wrong* here, that something about what I saw suggested a deeper meaning to why it was like this here.

I sensed in my mind something picking through my thoughts, as if my skull had been opened up and something was looking for whatever special thoughts, memories, and imagination that it fed on, and was diligently feeding: beetles picking the carcass clean.

Not unlike exactly what Frank had suggested.

"You do sense it, don't you?" Frank switched the tackle box to his right hand. It joined the pole as he put his left hand on my shoulder.

I lowered to my haunches, leaned my weight on my hand as I pressed the palm to the ground, an upper-limb kick-stand. I could swear I felt something pulsing warmly just below the surface. An image of the diseased moss covering bright red abrasions, or possibly just thick veins, came to me; I was tempted to plunge my eager fingers into the ground and find the source.

I shook the intrusion from my head, dismantling the skewed perceptions from my thoughts. Ridiculous! Standing up, I smiled, something I'm sure barely succeeded in accomplishing its intent.

"It's weird out here, sure. But you know me. I've never been one for forests. Nature's a ravenous bitch."

I gazed about some more, not letting my eyes rest on any one thing. Just a forest. Freaky empty patch here, but a forest nonetheless.

"That's enough for now." Frank smiled as well, but his smile was one of relief. As if he believed something had been accomplished by bringing me out here.

"Let's get something to eat," he said, turning to head back the way we had come.

"What? I thought you were going fishing?"

He actually laughed out loud with that one. "I did go fishing."

Was our conversation and curious conjecture the purpose of this oblique excursion?

"Let's head into town and get some lunch, Cisco." Urgency spurred his pace, the brittle crunch under his heavy boots sounding a rhythm that quickened one's heartbeat.

I was urgent to leave as well, to get out of this place—it gave me the creeps. Nature *was* a ravenous bitch. That and feeling my sense of time was, perhaps, way off.

"What time *is* it?"

5: Red Delicious

"You're the writer Derek Gray, correct?"

I turned to face the voice. Sounded muscular and resonant, as if a strong oak tree could speak, yet with the inflection of a female, for sure.

Alethea.

Frank and I had wandered up to the lone restaurant in this desolate scrap of land beyond the forest, a bland burgers and home fries' diner called Skunks. A grocery store imposed on the restaurant, no wall separating the two.

My thoughts moved beyond our recently aborted fishing jaunt, taking in the weirdness of it all. First the dreams and now the way my senses seemed lit by something, yet nothing distinguished itself, the sway of abysmal atmospheres inspiring synaptic shenanigans.

As I took in the whole of this handsome woman standing before me, Alethea's presence shook my senses in a good way. Her squared face, lifted by an exquisite jaw-line the envy of every two-bit boxer and champion alike, expressed a calm defiance, but the constructs within tantalized further. Playful yet mischievous eyes, jade sprinkled with chrome, glowing as mercury. Lips thick as plump worms—a bad metaphor, but it was what flashed in my head as I saw her (Frank's warped mindset seemed to be seeping into my own)—the plumpness in need of chewing—the bait—and me, captivated—the prey—accentuated by the deepest dimples I'd ever seen, age sinking them deeper, yet this was not a bad thing, not at all. A sleek, straight arrow English nose, offset by a slight upturn. Hair the color of an exploded rose, dark as blood at midnight, the slaughter still fresh, the blackness oozing, but enough light to tint it with this rich, delicious red.

She was something to admire, to visually consume and only hope there was enough to sate the eyes before the heart took over. Christ, I hadn't felt this kind of kick-drum driven arousal of the soul in years. It scared me, what I felt.

"Correct?" she said again, this time dipping her head, blackened strands of hair scooting out from behind the rim of red, flipping across her exotic face. Even her skin seemed unreal, a light dusting of red below the chiseled cheekbones. Cheekbones like the rest of her features, one of a kind, made for diving into the still waters of her silky skin.

"Perception from one of the locals, how quaint." I tried for amusing, but already felt I'd stumbled. Cut to the chase, boy!

"Alethea—correct?" I smiled and held out my hand. She took it, staring up at me, almost my height, just a hair off. With the dipping of her head she'd seemed shorter, but now she stretched, took my hand, hers warmer than I'd expected, and strong, but maybe that was just the shock of touching another. I expected it with the action, but the cold still lingered bone deep within me, despite the muggy overtones of the day. Nonetheless, her warmth distinguished itself as something more than natural, as if she was immune to the nasty freeze.

I was surprised anybody but an anthropologist could recognize me after the brain battering abuse of last night and the way it made me feel like I'd reverted to a Neanderthalian version of myself, dragging knuckles and carrying heavy bags under my eyes.

We stared for a moment before Frank interrupted it like a shard of mirror from the dream, this moment strangled by his ego.

"Frank Harlan Marshall. Pleased to meet you, Miss...Alethea..."

"Just Alethea. The pleasure's all mine." She took his hand and shook it, but her eyes only left me for a flicker, like flames showing off, dancing above the candle, with me as the candle upon which their dance was meant to be displayed.

I was sixteen again. What a fool, you'd think I would have

learned after all these years, but these sensations, these feelings: all who love never lose touch with them. Sometimes they hibernate, sometimes there's damage that makes them hide, but they are always there for those willing to allow themselves to breathe deeply and take a chance (again), possibly opening the gates to something special.

These thoughts made me giddy, or possibly it was the almost drugged remnants of the dreams as mixed with no real sleep. Here I was, thinking about love with a woman whom I had just met, though through her art I felt as if I knew her already. Yet I also understood that one's art was not always indicative of the person who created it. We are all individuals, and one's art is only a part of the crazy quilt fabric that is one's self. Of course, as with my art, Alethea's art seemed to be a direct extension of the actual person creating it and not, as with many creative individuals, the mastering of a certain skill. It was not an art by default. I'd noticed autobiographical elements in much of her lyrics. Hers was more an art by necessity, a crucial aspect of existence, like mine.

In one ring-laden hand—moonstone and amber and possibly black opal, all wrapped and set in intricate, purposeful designs— she carried a plastic bottle of Gatorade. In the other hand, adorned with equal enthusiasm and accompanied by snake-like bracelets, one of which had an Ouroboros inclination as the clasp set the tail into a flicked tongue mouth, she clenched an apple, about to take a bite. The clash of apple red and her deep red lips, as haloed by the blood red that encircled most of her face, tantalized in a dangerous way. The crack and tear, the too many teeth—another of my weaknesses exploited—and speaking again: "We should get together. Maybe I could help you better define that character from your latest novel that you've based on me."

She smiled coquettishly, enjoying the look of evasion into confirmation that skittered across my gaze.

"You know where I live. Drop by sometime."

She took another bite, her expression inquisitive, the force of her curiosity almost overpowering, much as, I'm sure, mine was registering with her.

Only a brief encounter, but I knew it would most definitely not be our last.

On the way back to Frank's house, Frank downshifted into cruelly playful interrogation.

"She's an odd one, eh?"

"Sure. Eclectic."

"You always like 'em different, don't you?" Frank, as usual, getting to the point, perhaps feeling like a mischievous joust, something he hadn't done since I'd been here. Maybe he was shaking out of the doldrums that had permeated his mood so far.

"You know me. Dime a dozen is good for a one off, but anything of substance is always gleaned from, as you like to say, the different women."

"But you know if you just hooked up with one of your dime a dozen beauties you'd probably have a relationship that lasted as opposed to the ones you've had."

I thought of my two marriages. My soul cringed at the memory of their finales, each one a new and exasperating form of mental train wreck.

But I also knew I needed more than casual beauty to drive my soul.

Doreen, wife number one, was probably the one I should have stuck with, with her shock of red hair (another redhead) and strong, so strong. But my immaturity and free-wheeling spirit cost me the best thing I'd ever had. The relationship with her now was cordial, actually better than cordial: she still did the cover artwork for my novels as well as the huge tree tattoo that filled the canvas of my back, celebrating my first novel, *Breathing Shadows*, a generational saga with teeth, the family being lineal descendants of a mythological presence that, while never clearly defined, was an integral part of their history, something that Frank had remarked about yesterday as I sweated, shirtless and swinging the axe. "You should be living out here with me, my friend. Your nature is closer to *this* nature than any city." Doreen had married soon after our relationship slammed into the wall, giving me no chance to try to correct my failings (again; I didn't blame her for her haste), but at least her husband was not a prick. Especially since our children, Claire and Dennis, were with her; beautiful kids, teenagers now—

how time flies when...well, it's not all fun, but it keeps flapping its wings—somehow they had avoided the pervasive insinuations of media and held onto some sort of sanity and sensibility. Even after my rock star trashing the hotel denouement to the relationship, me drunk again, what an embarrassment I was. Like a chimpanzee behind bars, I deserved everything that got flung my way during that down period in my life.

If I harbored any regret, which I do not allow myself to have, it would be that I wasn't there for them all the time. But I see them often and make the best of that time. They know I love them.

We all make choices, options open for reappraisal when one looks back, but the best one can do is realize that what has been done has been *done*, so deal with it, and make sure not to make the same mistakes—excuse me, the same *choices*—again.

Asia, my second wife, was not the madman taking the same step, repetition into insanity. Oh, no. She was definitely a different breed. Three years in the eye of the storm, a drug-addled sexual storm, she was a spoken word performance artist much like Lydia Lunch, the same grit and primal grunt, and the drugs, well, that overtook everything. At the end she left out of nowhere, just as she had come into my life. I'd only realized she'd left after I got the divorce papers, and the battle that ensued for everything I owned. That was a media circus that probably mentally inhibits me from marrying again.

Christ, she was a piece of work--pitch black spiky hair, a constant snarl across her thin lips, eyes that flared deep blue while always being rimmed in red like a total lunar eclipse, and a body like a panther on the prowl: sleek, agile, never relaxed. That whole scenario was the one time I'd really locked into the drug world in more than a passing manner. It almost killed me. Frank and I did the occasional excursions into mind-altering substances, but mostly we needed just to open our minds and reality was altered via our imaginations. Drugs never did either of us any good. Frank held them closer to his soul. I dipped in, took a swim, got out, dried off, and moved on.

That said, Frank despised everything about Asia.

Last I heard, she was in rehab, again. It was more a permanent residence at this point, which made headlines and kept her in the news, not that it really mattered. She'd done nothing of creative substance in a handful of years. I only hoped that rehab might actually work, but her history was engrained in her bones. It saddened me, but she was gone and as long as she wasn't asking or (more often) berating me for anything else, that was fine by me.

She was simply a part of my history now. My warped history.

I'd had plenty of other extended dalliances. A year with Jamaica Jennefer here, another year with supermodel Gina there, Darlene's southern fried romp 'n' roll for a spell. On and on, many more signposts on the relationship highway, all leading to dead ends.

I just figured I was destined to have solid friendships with women, some leading to physical companionship, but nothing leading to permanence. It seemed no winning hands were in the cards.

I kept drawing a joker.

Or maybe I was the joker...

"Some things..." I let it dangle. I couldn't deny who I was, what I liked, what I enjoyed in a woman. Even if it was not for permanence, women of intrigue, whose lives had been lived just to the left of the norm, always fascinated me.

"Some things never change." He smiled.

"What's to change? It's too much fun going on these emotionally, um, *stimulating* rides, anyway. Not that I expect anything with Alethea. And who are you to hand out advice? Three times married, all to the same woman..."

Carissa, a bleach-blonde starfucker. She kept coming back for more, even after incidents that made my break-ups look like minor disagreements. Some people seemed destined to destroy each other no matter how much they tried to avoid each other, rusted magnets that corroded hopelessly intertwined souls. In between all of the other women who wandered in and swiftly out of Frank's life, Carissa was a paradox: chaos as stability.

"And too many frivolous affairs and one-night stands to count," I continued.

Frank ignored the truth of his unruly existence, continuing on his wheedling path.

"You just want to get to know her better, eh? Character development, maybe?"

"Well, yeah…"

"Not in the biblical way, eh?"

"Well…I mean…"

Frank laughed. "Those breasts have got you in their sites."

I had to acknowledge that she did have some wonderful breasts, but not to this weasel. "You're just going to sink to crudity now, aren't you?"

"I wasn't being crude. When have you ever been one to avoid explicit observations? Those are some amazing breasts."

We wore stupid smiles on our faces as we wandered down the dirt road toward Frank's house. I actually forced myself not to look up at Alethea's house as we passed it, not wanting her to see the stupid smile on my face and understand what had inspired it.

6: Alethea's Haven

Later that day, as the sun made a swift getaway between the branches and behind the mountains, my brain fried from a few hours of writing on the laptop while Frank zoned out to the front room television downstairs, frying his brain cells in a less constructive manner, I decided it was as good a time as any to get a breath of fresh air, amongst other things.

"You okay if I head over and hang out with Alethea?"

"Yes, my son"—the words hobbled from Frank's lips, as if whittled from something ancient, forgotten—"don't you care about your daddy if you want to get your dick wet—"

"Shut up, old geezer! Put a lid on your dirty mind, would ya?"

"Yeah, yeah, well, I'm feeling a bit tired anyway. Might hit the sheets early, wouldn't be much company. Need some sleep, too many dreams not helping the matter."

This jostled my interest. "What kind of dreams?"

"I don't...I don't really know. It's like they're sketches. None of the people looks like the persons they're supposed to be representing. None of the familiar details have been added, yet their motivations and such are very much in sync with these people, and all these people from my past are gathering for something I cannot make out." He hesitated, the squirrelly, evasive look in his eyes hinting at knowledge of why these people from his past might all be gathering together, yet still avoiding explanations. "Sure, I got some more regular dreams, ones where the brain seems to be running wild, sex and stuff, but these dreams, these other ones, they wear me out. I wake up more tired than when I'd gone to sleep." He stared out the window. "It's become an obsession, these dreams. Been going on for a while."

A few nuthatches fluttered around a birdfeeder hanging from the bowing branch of a tree out front.

"I'm gonna feed those birds, get a bite, and go to bed. Sorry for all the excitement, but..." He continued to stare, as if the words would magically materialize, finger-written on the breath-fogged window in front of him, but nothing followed.

"Sounds like the dreams I had last night. Some of it nightmarish and freaky, but most of it was more defined, the women in my life making appearances, but still, even at that they were whittled into some monstrous version of themselves. Ultimately, it was cluttered and exhausting."

"Yeah, you look like shit. You could be a character from one of my novels, about to meet a grizzly death and welcoming it for all you've gone through up to that point." He smiled, obviously getting sadistic satisfaction out of this. "In your present state, I'm surprised Alethea had the courage to even talk to you."

"Thank you for the kind words, dear friend." I snarled at him, more mischievous than malicious. "As if you look like a prince. You could use a diet and some exercise, Pancho. Or should I call you 'Paunch-o?'" I patted him on the belly; it jiggled.

Back to the ancient, weathered voice: "I'll take your suggestions under consideration, my son. I'll start by lifting this bottle of rum to my lips a few times, then move on to the stairs, painfully lifting my creaking bones up to the bed, after which I will nod off, drooling and farting. After I feed those birds. If I have the energy."

"You are an inspiration to us all!"

Frank picked up a bag of bird food and headed out.

I followed but veered left. The early October eve snuggled into my bones. The jacket I wore was feeble defense to the vacillating weather up here. The cold had come on strong again, a notch or two on the downside of comfortable.

Alethea's house was an ungainly but fascinating blend of architecture. The side facing Frank's place seemed a jumbled array of angles and edges, nothing smooth, while toward the almost hidden front door, a nod to something archaic prevailed. It had more distinction, more personality, fraught with wooden wind-chimes that emitted sporadic padded rhythms that took on the cast of something tribal, a dream catcher, and an array of handiwork that brought faces out of the rich oak around the door. Strange, fascinating faces, almost human, maybe animal. I was reminded of Dr. Moreau's failed experiments. I glanced up to see Alethea at the door.

"Warmer in here," she said.

"I was just admiring the architecture, the art."

"Ah, yes, my friends from the spirit world. My friends from the realm of mythology and dreams. My true friends." She reached over and stroked one of the faces. It was a face that would have inspired dread under other circumstances. A face like her house, all edges, elongated, a man, perhaps, yet an animal struggled within, scratching to get out, the rough markings on his cheeks signifying as much. I realized my unease was unwarranted as the more I looked at it, the more I realized the face was one of humor, of buoyant naughtiness. A jester in need of an audience. I'd swear the smile widened at her touch.

"Come. Now. You're letting the heat out."

With the statement, I liked her more.

I entered, greeted by genuine warmth. The warmth in Frank's place seemed just enough to stave off cryogenic paralysis. In reality it was just barely enough heat, never too much, and sometimes the body wanted more. Here, the heat pleasantly engulfed me.

"The cold is coming on strong a bit early this year. Usually it hits hard in November. We're only at the beginning of October and it's starting to kick in with force. I don't expect it will last, we should see a few more warm days, but this is rather surprising." She smiled, handing me a mug. The heat was like an electrical charge, radiating from the cup to the flesh of my fingers, sliding along the phalanges and into the marrow. I felt them awaken.

"What is this?" I said, after sipping without delay. "It's interesting."

"It's my own special recipe, a mix of this and that meant to warm the soul. It's also good for my voice."

I took another sip and the honeywarm flavor glazed my mouth

and throat. I figured it would be very good for a vocalist.

I already knew I liked her a lot. The impression one gleans from the outside, especially with a public or somewhat public personality, is often skewed. With Alethea, the impressions I had gathered in the construction of Ashlyn Cage were on full display here, and intensified by her openness, the confidence and casual comfort in my company already, as if we were old friends and not just this day getting to know each other.

Stepping into a large den, the sudden inception of odors infused my nostrils and thoughts with delightfully conflicting data: sandalwood and jasmine mingled, dueling, heady aromas often thought of as masculine and feminine. Many a seduction has been set forth with these aromas as co-conspirators.

Along with the incense, flames writhed with resolute intent above colored candles—white, purple, red, and green. The flicker was steady, but animated, like a bee trapped in a jar. The candles lit the room with a brightness that rivaled the sun's natural radiance.

The odors and candles immediately fell by the wayside as I spotted shelves overflowing with books and ambled towards them. My novels were sprinkled amongst the fiction, mythology, folklore, paganism, philosophy, and over-sized art books. The fiction dovetailed directly into my favorites: Borges, Cypher, Hand, Vellirane. The other books also dabbled where I had dabbled. Stacks of books leaned and tottered precariously. Bookmarks jutted from some of the books, indicative of points of interest on a map, of something that touched her and might require rechecking. At least, that was my perception, remembering a few books I'd stuffed with torn paper, receipts and movie stubs as bookmarks.

A large, partially obscured photography book distracted me in a most peculiar way, what with a puce ribbon, much like Frank's and my award winning ribbons, draped over the cover, while resting comfortably within its black and white collection of photos.

But Alethea wandered deeper into the room, another distraction for my focus, and I was made to move away from the book and the puce ribbon which demanded attention, but would find none at this time. Perhaps later. Perhaps never.

A table next to a large recliner that looked like the perfect place to sink into for maximum comfort was sprinkled with more books, including a few tomes on "chaos magick," something titled *The Mythology of Nature*, another titled *Primal Vibrations: Sound Through the Ages*, and on top of the lot, *The Phenomenology of Sound*. The table was intricately carved, much as her porch. It all intrigued me.

I set my mug on a wooden coaster, one of many scattered along the tables and book shelves throughout the room, and picked up the phenomenology book, thumbing through it. Philosophy and more, a twist on phenomenology I had not explored, though some of the familiar names associated with phenomenology were included — Husserl (of course), Heidegger, Ravenscott — as well as some familiar though obscure names culled from fringe explorers of music — Ctrl/Alt/Delete, Merzbow, James Plotkin.

"Husserl. Didn't he used to sing for Black Sabbath?"

"Didn't everybody used to sing for Black Sabbath?"

We both laughed at that, a sad truth woven into the statement.

"How does phenomenology relate to sound?"

"Well, since it deals with the essences of everything, as channeled through our experiences in the world, my interpretation is that the sounds, the essences of sound itself, can maybe open doorways within us to experiences that we might never imagine. It's a matter of one's consciousness and experiences, beliefs, perceptions, the whole hodgepodge of ideas, ideals and obsessions that makes each of us tick."

I shook my head, yes, anything was possible. *I* could eventually sing for Black Sabbath…

Alethea nodded to the book in my hands.

"It's all grist for the mental mill. Anything that ventures into unfamiliar territory, be it sound itself or sound as that book explores it, everything from manipulated noise to silence, which never really is silent, there's always a core of vibration, of something that triggers an auditory reaction, I love that stuff. The world is vast and full of layers we cannot imagine. Both all around us as well as in our heads."

And maybe shouldn't imagine, I thought, thinking of Frank's present psychological status. I flashed to a famous quote by one of

Frank's favorite writers, H.P. Lovecraft: "The most merciful thing in the world…is the inability of the human mind to correlate all its contents." I kept it to myself, pointing to another book on her shelf, *Unnatural Architecture*, the cover of which featured a tree with too many branches, more like spider legs, and a door at the base, with a lock on it.

"Pissed off hobbit's abode?"

"More a dramatization of the genius loci of that tree, that place. Maybe the structure of the world can also alter our experiences, to some degree. Maybe…" She smiled, her face breaking into a huge grin that seemed to encompass the possibilities as well as the lunacy of it all.

I thought of how this related to my walk in the forest with Frank, and even the gist of his mental quandary.

"It's all just a matter of one's—"

"Perception," I said, holding up Aldous Huxley's mescaline-fueled *The Doors of Perception*.

"Among other things. Don't limit yourself, I say."

I thought of Frank's current mindset, the willingness of him being open to the possibilities, or perhaps the possibilities being opened to him—*for him?*—and his own personal, and obviously fractured, perceptions.

Huxley or Husserl or simply hubris gone mad.

7: Ashlyn Cage

Like a smoothly oiled machine, she shifted gears.

"So, Ashlyn Cage—why me?" There was no animosity, just curiosity.

No flinching from me as well: "I've been following your work for only a few years, catching up, reading everything I could about you, interviews—the whole deal."

"Cyber-stalking me, eh?" Her smile lacked malevolence. It was playful, as she had been the whole evening.

I shook my head. "No, not cyber or any other kind of stalking. I just find people fascinating, and those who dance along the fringes of popularity, those who do not succumb to the sick lure of celebrity, those who stick to their guns when it comes to their creativity, I find them the most fascinating. Since a lot of my characters are of this creative outsider mindset, somebody like you makes sense to me."

"You mean it wasn't just my breasts?"

I coughed and the warm tea-like drink tickled the back of my nostrils.

"Kidding," she said, all teeth, playful again. Devious, this one, an unhinged sense of humor, yet always in control.

"So, are you here now to more observe than anything else, to see what makes me tick, to help Ashlyn find her soul? Shall I move you into the guest room, just like Johnny Depp did with Hunter S. Thompson for the movie *Fear and Loathing in Las Vegas*, so you can get all the nuances down right, physically as well as mentally, to really get inside the character?"

"No, no, not that extreme, but to some extent, yes. I mean"—

no reason to deny anything, I knew she was being, and would be, completely open—"I have found the person I have gleaned from the music and history most intriguing. And, let's be honest, if you were somebody I didn't find physically attractive, I might not indulge the fantasy of Ashlyn any more than what she has already been." I paused, gauging if the path was truly clear and seeing no obstacles. "But the more I have gotten to know about you, and now, standing here in your house, talking to you, it heightens elements I've already had under consideration for Ashlyn. And yet, I am in all actuality just hoping to get to know you because I know there's a somewhat similar mindset here that I think would work for me as, well, as a potential friend, if nothing else."

"Or something more." Dimples again in full bloom.

"Well…"

"Don't stop now, you're on a roll, Derek."

"I just find you intriguing and want to know more about you. If it enhances the character, well…"

The words stalled, my head reeling in a good way.

"Are you finding what you want?"

What did I want?

"Yes, now Ashlyn will have this really wicked sense of humor to play off of as well."

"You can only go so far anyway. You can never really capture one's soul on paper, no matter how hard you try."

"You've read my book, *The Soul, Extinguished*, correct?" I'd seen the book on her shelf, I knew she had. She nodded, yes. "Don't you think Paul Schayles pretty much exhibited all of the heart and soul of a real person?"

"Oh, I'm not denying the essence. To a point…"

"Come now! My most fully realized creation and you don't think he is the epitome of a real person, even if he is fictional?"

"The reality is never as extravagant as the fictional. Of course, if a writer included all of the minutiae, we'd get lost in the mundane. All novels would be thousands of pages long. But, beyond the exterior, it's the interior lives that can never be completely experienced through fiction, or any other art." She went to sip from her mug, gave it an odd look—it must have been empty—and continued. "Our thoughts are 'on' at all times. And they are unlimited, ever-shifting, mad, deeply personal, of course, and often perverse or crude or quite base, if one is really honest, which even inside, most people deflect *that* line of thinking as well."

"That's too literal. That's impossible."

"Correct. But it's also the difference between a character and, well, us: humans. Our interior world is so complex, it might be *necessary* to leave it inside and never reveal all of it. If we let it all out the world would implode with the madness that romps through our personal thoughts. You can get close, though. That pure, uninhibited, free-flowing monologue is attempted by some writers."

"Burroughs?"

"Sure, Burroughs, to some extent, but his is more a drug-induced perspective, and the addition of drugs changes everything. Maybe J.G. Ballard."

"I was going to suggest Ballard. *Crash* is so internalized, I remember reading sections and thinking, I can't believe he wrote that, I can't believe he allowed us into such a personal and perverse line of thinking."

"Honest. Not perverse. Pure honesty."

"Right, honest."

"Scary thought, that."

"Very," I said. "But I also remember thinking that it was perfect, because it was completely uncensored."

"But even there—"

"How about the interior monologues of Frank's Average Joe?" Though Frank was more a meat and potatoes writer, when he was on, it was something to behold. The Average Joe interior monologues were chilling.

"Yes, actually, you might be onto something there. I've only read two of those books. They were too much for me."

We paused, both inhaling deeply, the music in the background, so far away.

"Back to Paul Schayles," she said, "you can get close, but no matter how open a person is, you might still only derive something that rubs up against the purity of one's being."

I thought I'd created some characters that I, as well as many readers and even some critics, would deem as complete a person as possible within the realm of fiction writing, yet what she said made sense. Still, it frustrated me, my ego battered a bit.

"I don't believe in candy-coating anything, Derek." She searched my eyes, playfully punching my shoulder.

"Ah, no worse than some of the reviews my work has gotten." I smiled, not really insulted by anything she had said, more understanding that it made sense and that only made it a challenge for the development of future characters. Annoyance as prompt to growth.

I wondered how I would add this element to developing the character of Ashlyn Cage, and then thought to drop it for now and just talk to the reality that was Alethea.

I also wondered about Frank and his Average Joe interior monologues, how he got them so right, or at least right in the sense of how I would assume a madman such as Average Joe would think. Maybe going to those dark places in his head had shaken him to the marrow.

A chill massaged the hairs on the back of my neck. I took another drink from the mug and shook those thoughts from my head.

We continued for a while like this, and finally sat down as well, a true tit-for-tat conversation, something of substance and thought-provoking. One of the best, most invigorating to no end conversations I'd had in years. Fairly amazing since I'd just met her. But we seemed of a similar mindset, and this mindset was something that entwined as we got to know each other better.

At about three in the morning I headed toward the door, in need of sleep, not really wanting to leave and still rolling with it, but she also was noticeably winding down. It reminded me of the nervous deceleration of a music box, the end creeping up to sweep it into silence.

"How long are you here, Derek?"

"Not sure. Frank's in a bad way in his brain, and another friend of ours we haven't seen in many years is supposed to show up any day now. I'd say there's a good two or three weeks at least."

In her best southern twang, she said, "Y'all come back now, y'hear," and winked.

"Most certainly." I did a funky bow and put my hand out. She took it and pulled me close to her. I was immediately aware of her heat. We hugged and her heat made me want to stay and lay my head on a pillow next to hers, even if sleep was all that was on the agenda.

8: Average Joe

Seems we can't avoid him, now that he's been brought back into our lives. Even if he is not, as yet, officially here.

I entered the house, expecting Frank to be asleep, but could hear the television blaring from his bedroom.

I heard him laugh and made my way upstairs, wondering if he had already slept, or if he'd chosen to ride out the night, avoiding the sandman and postponing any appointments with his personal demons.

Atop the stairs, I turned the corner to see his patchwork bedroom. The so-called second floor was more an attic with a window. I had to hunch down a bit to avoid the ceiling. Surprisingly, there was also another room up there, which Frank had converted into a study, where he did all his writing: a computer with a large monitor sat on a desk, along with reams of paper as Frank only edited hardcopy printouts, never one to utilize the computer in this much more simplified, "but lazy," he would say, manner. There were also many books and magazines, used for research, or distraction.

Frank laughed.

"Did you just wake up? Tell me you've spent quality time with the sheep, counting, cuddling or…?"

"I thought I'd drop, but am inclined to push it, I guess. Not wanting to let my dreams run free." He hadn't turned to me, concentrating on the screen.

My initial assumptions had been correct.

I recognized the movie. Izzy had written and starred in three movies, of which *Communication Breakdown* was the most popular.

It dealt with a new Middle Eastern country establishing its own place in the world as well as its own language—which was straight-up English, yet translated to convey different meaning--to ridiculous ends, amidst the romantic hi-jinks at an international convention for peace. It included a surprising dose of seriousness that was side-swiped by many skits of such politically incorrect nature as to warrant its banning in some of the more sensitive cities.

Most just found it outrageous: the unrated DVD sales went through the roof.

Frank patted the bed, welcoming me to watch with him. Since it was one of the better scenes—well, within the kingdom of tastelessness, it was prime Izzy—I decided to sit for a few and maybe see how Frank really was doing.

We sat and watched the scene unfold:

Sheik Ratalandrol (Will Ferrell), from a podium: You fucking American swine deserve the worst of what we can bring you, filthy pig fuckers. Capitalist cocksuckers.

Translator (Bill Murray): We want nothing more than universal peace and love, democracy and hope, that the United States and Hateamericanistan can forge a relationship that will last eternally.

Reporter Clark Bent (Izzy): You gotta be kidding me, did you hear that load of—

Reporter Lois Armcandy (Reese Witherspoon): Beautiful. Absolutely beautiful. There is hope in the world.

Sheik Ratalandrol: Annoying American swine is the national pastime in Hateamericanistan. You cheap pig fuckers should all die in a sty of our shit, assholes!

Translator: We know that forging this friendship will help bring unity to our nations, and peace to the world.

Reporter Clark Bent: Lois, something is very wrong. I know they are a new nation with their own language, but I think somebody's pulling the wool over...

Clark looks at Lois. She has a tear running down her cheek.

Reporter Lois Armcandy: You never understand new things, Clark. You never give anything a chance. This is the most powerful moment in our lives and your inherent anti-Middle Eastern prejudice cannot accept that this new nation really wants to work with us in establishing a peaceful world. You are a mean person.

Clark Bent: I have never expressed any prejudice toward Middle Eastern cultures.

She looks hard at him, eyes narrowing, wiping the tear with much aplomb—take that!

He rolls his eyes, recomposes himself, hands on her shoulders, steadying her, and gazes deep into her eyes.

Reporter Clark Bent: You slimy piece of ostrich mucus. Stick your head in the garage of your ass and kiss your bowels while I puke on your miserable naïve ways.

Shocked, Lois Armcandy stammers: H-How can you be so—

Reporter Clark Bent, interrupting: What, my dear? Oh, I'm sorry, I'll get the translator to translate what I said, because it was the deepest of love that I wish you and I will have forever, with babies and...

Frank and I were rolling at that point. Inanity never was quite as fun as when a friend was involved. And this was just bad.

"You have a good time over there?"

"Yeah. Yeah, she's intriguing, for sure. She makes the engine of my brain hum merrily along, gears in full on contemplation mode."

"And your dick?"

"Christ, back to this? You are a decrepit pervert, aren't you?"

"No, I'm just that part of your conscience that speaks the truth. I take by your answer you didn't get any."

"You, my tubby friend, are beyond help. And no, I didn't engage in anything more than excellent conversation, but I'm sure I'll be seeing her again. Not that tongue wrestling is on the agenda, but—"

"Admit it. She totally fits into what you like."

"Didn't we already have this conversation?"

"Yes, but now you've had some time to get to know her—"

"Shut up and get to sleep. Don't wake me until noon, for all I care. I'm fried."

I went downstairs, tossed a few logs in the wood stove, miffed by the faded quality of the name—Bradfo...—and curious how it seemed a bit fuller, yet still rubbed out. And wasn't the "o" completely faded when I checked yesterday?

I shook my head, chalking it all up to exhaustion. I would welcome the sandman with open arms.

I was up at seven, of course. The scattered debris of mad dreams pestered my waking thoughts, but at least this time the discomfort did not linger. That said the overcrowded yet dissipating thoughts inserted snippets of Alethea into their freewheeling disorder. It felt like my being awake so early was similar to when a person is connecting with another person and that initial spark makes sleep and pretty much everything else outside of breathing and blinking secondary to the blossoming connection.

A possible side effect of falling in love? I didn't want to put that label on what I was feeling, but there was a definite attraction. Love, if it showed up, would probably ambush anything good anyway, so let it be and just roll with getting to know her better.

I was tired, sure, but I was also somehow weirdly refreshed. Must be an outlook thing.

I also noticed Frank out front smoking a cigarette, dark circles creating a moat around his eyes and the pensive look they flashed. I wondered what beasts guarded the orbs or if the orbs were simply trapped, unable to escape, because of the moat.

"Frank, you get any sleep?" Stretching at the door.

Frank continued to smoke his cigarette, as if he didn't hear me.

I exited the house and walked toward him.

"Hey, Pancho. You sleep? You okay?"

Frank turned to me, a smile pasted on his face and fighting through the ever pervasive gloom. He seemed quite off. And here I thought he might've been shaking out of his funk.

"I don't think my mind believes in sleep anymore. It's the only way it can avoid the dreams. It's taking a stand for its livelihood." He smiled again, despair laced with resignation, maybe.

"Didn't the pot from the other night alleviate any of your restlessness?"

"Just a bit, but the dreams that night—whew! Don't ask me to do that again. Any suggestions of self-imposed medicinal marijuana use should be scattered to the wind. Didn't help that reality had already been getting dicey."

Frank tilted his head, eyes squinting against the morning sun, as if he was trying to burn something within, burn it away.

"You said something the other night about your horrors coming back to haunt you. You never really explained this statement. What did you mean?"

Frank visibly pursed his lips in avoidance, the effort bringing out a lattice of wrinkles all around it. I was reminded of a mummy's stitched shut mouth.

"Talk to me, bud. How long has it been since we've been ruining each other's lives? Well, let's keep this merry-go-round spinning." I put my hand on his shoulder. The muscles felt knotted, big as plums, made of iron.

"It's not... It's not the mystery of nature that is what I deal with in my novels, you know? Not exactly. It's the soulless avariciousness of nature. It's how, by undefined magic or mental degradation, being in that environment, out within the forest, things come alive that one would normally catalogue as hallucinatory, of a dream foundation, and in my case--ours to be truthful--more evidence of a very wild imagination. But..." He paused, searching for something more, then completely stopped, sucking hard on the cigarette, cauterizing his imagination as if it was a gash he wished forever to seal up.

Frank's mention of magic grabbed my attention. A second mention of magic in less than half a day, what with Alethea's belief that magic abounded in our world. His take on nature was a philosophical caveat, one of which I kind of agreed. Things happen in forests that are sometimes never explained, and even more so, never revealed. It holds secrets, but those with a limitless imagination leaning toward the fantastic can sometimes pick up on that which lurks in the peripheral.

Unless, as Frank did in the transitional Average Joe novel, *Black Eden*, the peripheral moved to center stage. Evidence of Average Joe's death was never confirmed; Frank left the possibilities open-ended.

I often thought the forest assimilated Average Joe's essence, his evil. With the conversations of the last few days and reminiscences from the birth of the Sinister Nature series, a shifting of perception seemed in order. It seemed now that the forest had had a hand in the nurturing of the evil that resided within Average Joe, since his motivation, though more resolute, featured much of the chaos inherent in the bogus tranquility of a forest. That is, if one believes there are unexplained events, ideals, conspiracies and such in nature.

It was all fodder for deeper conversations on subjects most people wouldn't even consider. Ah, the hodgepodge mindset of the fantasist.

"How does this relate to…to the horrors coming back into your life? Does being out here with nature so near make you uneasy? Hell, you could live anywhere, you know. Maybe you need to get back to the chaos of the city."

"No, it's not as if I could live anywhere else, Derek. Sometimes everything within one's life, everything is with a purpose, and part of my purpose is to be here now. And whatever is to follow, well, maybe I don't have a say in how it takes shape. It's not like when I'm writing a novel. What happens here is not of a choice, it is to be experienced."

"But if…" I was at a loss. I could explore the determinism mumbo-jumbo that he suggested, but that wasn't a place either of us had expressed as possible before. I suppose digging in and finding out why he even considered this belief a possibility now might pull out some answers, but as with everything so far, the exercise was akin to pulling teeth with chopsticks. I decided to stay on track.

"What horrors are coming about, Frank? You're acting like you have no say in anything when it's your life, you got a say. Still, what horrors, what's up?"

Again with the deep drag, but this one with a look in his eyes, as if the cogs were slipping into place behind them, and he was going to try to finally find a way to open up and share with me.

"It's more like…the most recent novels that are inspiring my dread. The forest near me, I've wandered, I've even awakened a couple times out there"—head nod to our left: the forest—"not knowing how I got there, yet feeling like it's all with a purpose."

As if responding to Frank's head nod, or possibly his words, a sound as if something large was shaking the trees resonated from the forest, from a place deep within. A place we could not see, and could not confirm or dispel as to what was doing the shaking.

Close to them, the wind slept, offering no answers.

Frank continued as if he didn't even hear the sound. I had a passing thought that it might be because it was familiar to him, the mysterious whims of the forest, this forest; this place.

"I'd wake up and feel the dread heavy on my shoulders, a vulture about to feast on my head, my thoughts. I sense the mysteries I have incorporated in my fiction, those about nature and its sinister ways. I feel like nature is letting me know I am more than correct, and, at that, it's welcoming more observations, maybe something of the flesh, not just my mind. Do you understand?"

I felt the ground below me quiver, or at least something that related more to a quiver than to a quake. Possibly a pulse. It felt soft, almost liquid. Not solid like the hard dirt that I was standing on. An indescribable sound accompanied it, the rhythm so low I heard it more in my body than through my ears, but there was something. I shuffled my feet and the sensation faded.

"Not exactly, but I got a feel for it," I said, scratching my neck. Something's up, Frank's mind was fractured and in need of a vacation, without worry. My friend was slipping in a bad way.

To top that off, this place was starting to really freak me out.

I also got the impression again, because of the monotone drone of his delivery, that he understood completely what or why these things were happening. As if he had worked it all out, recited it over and over in his head, yet still did not want to let me in. I thought if he just got it all out, completely, maybe we could work past his depression, move forward. Have some of our usual fun.

"It's like," he paused, continued dully, "everything I have ever written about the evil in nature is on a collision course with some kind of impossible meeting with my previous creation, Average Joe. That's why I called you, what with Izzy on the way."

"What are you talking about? How does he have anything to do with Average Joe?"

He looked up at me, surprised. "You know I based Average Joe on Izzy, right?"

I'm sure I squinted hard at him. "What the hell *are* you talking about?"

He laughed, a raspy scraping of his throat. "C'mon, Derek. You should get it. You know how I've always described Average Joe: no distinctive features, brown hair, brown eyes, average height and weight, nothing to leave an impression, yet an impression, albeit a confused one, always left in the aftermath of his murders: 'I saw a guy hanging out, kind of suspicious,' 'What did he look like?' 'Just your average guy, think his hair was black, a little taller than you—' 'No, he was shorter than this guy, and his hair, I think it was brown, shoulder length—' 'No, it was short-cropped...'"

"Your point?"

"When Izzy first started doing stand-up, before we'd met him, I remember seeing him on Letterman a few times and thinking something about him radiated an average Joe kind of vibe, like he would be a cool guy to know, yet one would never really know him. An enigma." He dragged deep on the cigarette, as if the smoke were a means of sustenance. "I based the foundation for the Average Joe books on our friend, Izzy, because that enigmatic quality would be the perfect mask for a murderer. Meeting him only magnified these points, even with his over-the-top persona, because underneath, he was just your average Joe."

I had to think about Alethea and how Ashlyn Cage was the direct response to her, and now that I had met her, how the impressions were similarly magnified.

"Wow. I'd never realized this. Did you ever tell Izzy?"

"No." He paused, shifted uncomfortably. "It was never necessary to tell anybody this. Well, I thought I'd told you, but apparently I hadn't. And since Average Joe was such a nominal blank, no one ever made the connection."

"So, what you're saying is that you've had some kind of off the wall experiences recently, including sleep-walking—"

"You know I've never sleep-walked in my life until recently." He stared into the forest again.

The forest remained silent.

I continued, "You've had these experiences that somehow

coincide with your fiction, and you think that—what?—since Izzy is on the way that Average Joe is on the way, or what?"

"I suppose that's as good an observation as any." He dropped his cigarette on the dirt, stamped it out with his boot.

Perception, something I dealt with on a regular basis in my novels, was definitely getting a workout here.

9: The Tightening of the Noose

I spent the rest of the morning sketching out some details for the next novel on my laptop. I made a file titled "Alethea_Ashlyn" and typed a few pages of notes, meshing the two personalities as one, a person who might relate to the real person but had most of her soul buried in the mind of a quirky fantasist: me.

While I worked, the relative quiet at Frank's place disorientated me. I was used to a ruckus, phone calls and such, music blaring as purposeful distraction, washing out the street sounds from below my condo, or just opening all of the windows and letting those sounds work their way into my psyche.

Frank remained upstairs, playing DVDs to pass the time, the volume low, more like the midnight chatter of insects. I could tell what the latest one was, though: another of Izzy's cinematic exploits, *Night of The Cooking Dead*, in which he and Will Ferrell played dueling chefs, one of whom resorts to murder to win an Italian cooking competition. It included the classic blurb, "Just add garlic," as a tagline, a reference to a backstage murder at the competition. After the beheading of an assistant and filling a pot of penne with blood as all tomatoes had been misdirected to a pastry competition, Ferrell's character blurts, "Just add garlic," amidst shock and grumbling stomachs. *The Iron Chef*, as perceived by George Romero.

I made my way upstairs just after noon, in need of sustenance. Maybe head to an actual town and get something real to eat, not the limited culinary exploits of Skunks. Many varieties of burgers, sure, but burgers were not a staple of my diet. Boone was only 21 miles away. Though the roads were pot-holed and precarious, something that didn't land like a rock in my belly should make the trip worthwhile.

"Chow, Pancho. It's time to eat. Let's head out to Boone, get something more exciting than a burger."

"You need to get outta dodge already, eh? Place getting to you?"

"Sure, get outta dodge, pardner, and save my stomach from another greasy feast."

I couldn't read the look in Frank's eyes. He had turned the movie off, slipped the denim jacket on, and was going through the motions of getting ready, but there was something in his eyes that left me unclear as to how he felt about my proposition. I thought he would appreciate something besides grease and whatever came with the grease, but then again in his present condition, maybe grease was his life-blood.

We drove to Boone along a one-way strip of asphalt that cut through the trees. The trees eventually dispersed, trailing us in the rearview mirror as the borders filled with infertile, blotchy farmland. Even the livestock seemed to sag dejectedly as we sped by.

Boone was a pleasant town, a place sprinkled with art galleries and multi-cultural restaurants, a clean, thriving environment. Reminded me of Healdsburg, just north of San Francisco, where Doreen had chosen to settle down after the divorce. The kind of place that thinks it's the best place in the world and if you don't get it, well, that's your loss. At least it didn't shove its mightier-than-thou ego in your face as did much of Oregon.

I got it enough to know it would be good for a visit, a quick meal, maybe pick up some groceries at the Green Earth Foods store, but nothing more. Nonetheless, it felt good to be amongst the hustle-bustle of people again.

We parked in front of a place called Sharon's California Cuisine, a lively café swarming with people who looked fit and ready for the day. We stumbled out of the car, looking as if we'd just crawled out of a cave.

Didn't matter to them. The hostess was all shiny white teeth and sparkling ocean blue eyes, and sat us near the front window, apparently not afraid that our dour appearances would scare off any potential customers.

The whole time I was taking in the scenery, my peripheral vision had noticed Frank's teeming agitation.

"What's up? You wanted to 'get outta dodge' for a bit."

"No. You wanted out. I guess I was wrong to allow this excursion away from…" He fidgeted, as if the chair was laced with nails, or perhaps the niceties of the locals was like an attack of mosquitoes.

"Pancho, relax."

"How am I supposed to relax when it…"

He looked genuinely perturbed.

"Define 'it,'" I said.

He stopped his skittish behavior and stared at me. I could sense the heat of his trepidation.

Again: "Define 'it.'"

"The forest. That place back there. What do you think I've been talking about? The ambience, fercrissakes. I know you sense something, too."

He put his hands up to his ears, as if he was blocking a horrible sound that only he could hear.

"Not here," I said, tapping my fingers nervously on the Formica table top. "I got nothing but hunger here. And you haven't been talking clearly about much of anything. Care to start now?"

A slim waitress in tight black slacks and a blouse the same burgundy hue as the restaurant's décor sidled up to our table, setting down two menus, and almost sang as she said, "How're you gentlemen today? Can I get you started with a drink?"

Frank lowered his hands but squirmed uncomfortably. The waitress remained composed, though a sliver of anxiety lodged itself in her wary eyes.

"Corona for me." I looked at Frank again. He didn't seem as though he wanted to participate. "Make that two," I said, smiling weakly at her. She returned a smile of equal wariness and walked away.

"Pancho." Then deciding this was no time for nicknames forged in the frivolities of our pasts, "Frank. What are you doing?"

"Can't you sense it? It's calling to me."

"The forest? Christ, buddy, you need to calm down."

But calming down was not in the cards. Frank stood up sharply, hands to his ears, his chair crashing to the floor. Our waitress, returning with our drinks, lost her already subdued smile and hesitated.

"We need to go, Derek. It needs me closer to it. *It needs me.*"

When Frank had delved deep into drugs, the paranoia had slaughtered any signs of sensibility, had made him act and react much as he seemed right now. I had to wonder if he had partaken in something heavier than pot, though with his remarks about the dreams inspired by the pot from a couple days back, I had to think not.

He stomped out of the restaurant, barreling past patrons and waitresses with abandon; a wide birth parted as he left. I apologized to the waitress, "Sorry, he's been under the weather, sorry..." not sure really what to say, blabbing to fill the space, as if she cared. I'm sure she was simply happy to have us gone.

At the car, I grabbed Frank by the arm and said, "Frank. Stop this. Talk to me."

Though his hands had moved away from his ears, he shook his head violently, as if trying to dislodge something from within.

"I did. I am talking to you, Derek. I can't...I can't do this."

"Eat out?"

"Eat here. It's too far from..."

"The forest."

"Yes." Again with the steely glare. "From that place."

Frank closed his eyes and shook his head one more time, stopping as abruptly as he had started. He got into the car and pouted. This was so out of character for him, even during his worst times. I thought it best just to get back to his house, alleviate whatever was disturbing him, while realizing I was only feeding his psychosis. Some friend I was.

During the drive, he turned to me and said, "When was the last time you spent any time in a forest, in nature, beside yesterday's brief stay?"

"Colorado. Two winters ago. Angeline—"

"The model?"

"Yeah, nice girl, good for a few laughs, that's all."

"Well," he paused, seeming to calm down the closer he got back to his house; the closer he got back to the forest. He put his hand on my wrist, gripped hard and spoke with hushed, conspiratorial tones: "You're in for something different here, if you keep your senses alert. This place will eat you alive, Derek. It's fuckin' evil, friend. A hub of spiritual and psychological emptiness. And it's hungry."

There, he laid it out, even more clearly than yesterday. Which made no sense. Maybe the years of drug use had finally caught up with him. Paranoia amped to the nth. I actually wondered if I was going to get him back, get Frank Harlan Marshall, my life-long friend, back.

I also wondered if we should both just leave, maybe wean him off the bad vibes, utilize my place in San Francisco for virtual rehab, since there didn't seem to be any drugs involved; it was all psychologically inspired. After all, we don't let our true friends wallow without throwing a rope, a lifesaver.

Before I suggested this, he said, "No. We need to go back home. Everything" — without conviction, but under a veil of equanimity that had been missing the whole time I had been up here — "everything will be fine. It will be fine."

I was thrown by the fact that his remarks seemed a direct response to my thoughts, but didn't let that deter the question that begged asking. "Fine? What about the evil?"

"Everything…will be fine. I know what needs to be done now. I've known all along."

There was no sign of conviction as he said this. More like resignation. He stared with deadeye dread at the oncoming forest. These supposedly comforting words were spoken as if he were a doomed man, sitting in the electric chair, yet *welcoming* the electricity onslaught.

He said this as if he was trapped.

If he knows what needs to be done, I wish he'd tell me. I wish he'd do whatever it was that needed to be done. I didn't know how much more of any of this I could take.

10: Stove-Top Mysteries

After a few hours, it seemed he had completely depressurized since we'd gotten back, as if the weight of the world, as well as Venus and Mars, had been lifted from his shoulders, but I needed confirmation. He seemed much as he'd been the whole time so far, not himself, but not the pseudo drug-crazed madman at the restaurant.

"You better now?"

"When Izzy shows up, it will all make sense."

"Whatever you say." I needed to be away from him for a bit, even if I wanted to help. Maybe Izzy's appearance would set things back on a more reasonable path, which was in itself a preposterous thought. "Alethea asked me over, she's got rough demos that she's working on, would like my feedback."

"So, you're a music critic as well, huh?"

"No, just feedback, like I do with my novels while they're in progress, with each draft. Like you should let me do with your latest novel. Let me read what you've completed so far with the novel that's hit the wall, maybe I can see something to help get you over that wall. Maybe I can somehow help."

"You know me better than that, Derek."

"Right." I had to shake my head. "Nobody reads it until it's completed. Period."

He actually smiled at this. "You learn well."

"Okay, I'm gonna head next door."

Frank leaned against the wood stove, which was amazingly not required this evening. The cold had scattered, the heat had crawled in and made itself comfortable, like a cat to your lap, no premise to foreplay, just taking over. I can't say I minded.

That's when I noticed the writing etched into the wood stove: Bradfor...

"What the fuck, you messing with me?" I tapped a finger on the wood stove.

Frank turned to see what had sparked my ire: the almost completed name.

"I haven't done anything. What are you talking about?"

Frank attentively watched me run my fingers over the letters, confirming their veracity; making them real.

"These letters. I mentioned it offhand the other day. The way..." But I was miffed. The way what? If Frank wasn't messing with me, and he has been known to distribute some rather devious practical jokes, then what exactly was up?

Frank's lips curled up slightly, as if he understood. "See, it's this place. It's getting to you as well. Or maybe it's showing you stuff you didn't know was there."

"What is that supposed to mean?"

"I told you, this place gets to you. Maybe" — rubbing the letters with the enthusiasm of Aladdin — "maybe this is showing you something about..." He continued to rub them, probably hoping a genie with all the answers would appear, or at least one with three wishes to grant.

I bent down and inspected the letters. There was no final letter. No indication that one had ever been there. And yet, just yesterday, there was no "r" as well, and now there was. Impossible.

Frank had to be messing with me.

"All right, Frank. Whatever you're doing, I'll go along for the ride. Better be a good payoff, though." I patted him on the shoulder; the plum had turned into an apple. I pictured him as Quasimodo in a few days.

Frank looked at me as if I was crazy, yet I also perceived a kind of understanding in his look as well. As if he really thought something was taking form here and was getting nearer.

Abruptly changing the subject, he said: "I got a call from Izzy earlier. He'll be here soon, maybe tomorrow."

I'd heard no phones ringing. Cell phones were fairly useless out here; the land line was the only real connection to the world beyond. I would have heard the phone ringing.

"When did he call? I've been here the whole time and we've had no calls."

"You questioning me, Cisco?"

"No, but don'tcha think I would've heard the phone?" Trying not to seem annoyed, yet annoyance itched at the back of my brain, under the skin of my scalp and spreading through me.

"Yeah, well..."

As if that was enough of an answer to satisfy me, but with this whole conversation, loose ends and hinting at more, I knew making sense was beyond my ken this evening.

"Our vibrations are getting nasty," he said, in his best Hunter S. Thompson. Or at least his best Johnny Depp interpretation of Hunter S. Thompson, I thought, uneasy with the intrusion on Alethea's Thompson reference with Frank's reference now. Not sure why, but something was way out of kilter and moving further out of kilter with exponential resolve.

"Very," I said, heading out the front door. "Very freakin' nasty."

11: Musique Concrète

Alethea welcomed me with more of her warm, tea-like drink, and a warmer hug. Despite the all-around heat, both were more than appreciated. I knew, no matter what, I was glad Frank had called me up to help him deal with his demons, because meeting this amazing woman was worth the weirdness that lingered at his place.

"This sounds more like the music you made on the last Dark Angel Asylum disc than your solo work."

"Musically, they are related, though no street samples here, they're all taken from nature. A musique concrète foundation has been a major part of my solo work as well. But you also have to remember, this is the raw material. There's much work to be done before it's finished. Before it is abandoned," she said, back of her hand to her forehead, faux dramatics that made me smile.

The sounds seemed deep, distant, yet all encompassing. I thought these were only field recordings, yet there was a pulse, a reverberation inherent to the natural sounds. I had a moment's awareness of a similarity to the sounds that I had heard—*and strangely felt*—this morning, while talking with Frank. I wondered what she had done, how much she had already manipulated these sounds, but was side-tracked by her voice. It had a quality like glass being blown to the brink of collapsing, yet a strength pushed the sound out of her without concern; and it was sound, not language, not yet at least. More an accompaniment to the vibrant, mysterious life playing out on the field recordings.

As the song worked through minor progressions inspired more by variance of volume than actual structure, and a thickening of the vocals seemed to point toward a climax, it scrabbled at the precipice before tumbling back without true release. There was tension, but not an unpleasant tension; a promise of something more, but that something more was, as yet, unrevealed.

"Wow. I've spent time in studios with a couple bands while they constructed loud, brutal noise: one metal band, one power electronics group. In both cases, nothing of the depth you have here ever came through."

"Song structure has never been the point with me."

"I know, it's just, hearing the material at this stage, and your vocals—Jesus—it's almost as if you can bend your vocal cords to fit the moody tenor of the sounds."

"Not bad. I knew you would be able to pick up on the nuances."

"Well, not sure if I've picked up on nuances, don't feel let down if most of my observations are tainted by my lack of true knowledge as to the formation, construction, and delineation of sounds. Especially at this early stage, with these recordings."

"Oh, no. I just knew that your mindset would be able to encompass all I am trying to do here or at least be open to whatever was presented. Eventually, as I work through the tracks, I'm curious if you will see the big picture."

Track two started, similar yet somehow completely different. I decided just to speak my mind as I listened, tempted to let my interior monologue out, that part of a character Alethea claimed is never let out. An attempt at stream-of-consciousness, but more stumbling than streaming, which might actually be more honest.

"It's the same on some levels, yet very different. Like, maybe…the same location on different nights?"

I raised an eyebrow, seeing if I was right.

"Not quite. But not bad."

The track evolved and got quite loud, a similar escalation in volume as the first track that seemed impossible if created by simply the equipment, yet because I did not know the equipment that well, maybe I was correct. It didn't sound like simply turning a volume knob, it seemed more organic and alive. Things thickened again, but it had grown so different from the first track that I thought my initial remark about them being the same location on different nights foolish. I looked at Alethea who held her empty mug in both hands, deep in concentration.

I was compelled to continue my input, but was also so fascinated by the sounds that I did not want to miss anything. Any thoughts of letting go and getting this out in a stream-of-consciousness manner were dammed up by the sheer audacity and originality (or possibly the origin itself) of the sounds. My mouth was also dammed up, bereft of words. The character's growth already stunted.

Three minutes into the track, a sound that was vocal but very animal rose from the din, and it had such ferocity that it startled me. The voice, which could only be Alethea's, unless a coyote, bear, or perhaps Bigfoot had crossed paths with the recorder, coiled into something almost human, and I was made to sit straight-backed and slack-jawed at the transition. As the song wound down, a distinct nod to purposeful entropy, something animal, or at least with the primal presence of an animal, squiggled through the speakers again and warbled in a way that seemed both pained and *expected*. I was getting so many perceptions, it was filling my brain with so many possibilities, that I had to force the mug to my lips, just to close my stupefied jaw.

"How...?" I looked at her, wondering how anybody could create something so personal from something that seemed so alien.

"The ancient Greeks believed everything was vibration, a kind of celestial vibration, and the sounds that emanated from instruments was less a result of the musician and more a translation of fragmentary pieces of these sounds. At least, that's my understanding."

"But if there are no instruments..."

"Sounds are everywhere at all times. Even silence has an undercurrent of, for lack of a better word, 'self.' When I make my excursions into the forest and make my recordings, my mindset is also aligned to this kind of thinking. Therefore, for those open to the true verisimilitude of sound, pure sound, and what it actually is, the gist of an unknown language is presented. A language of the heavens" — she raised her right hand to the ceiling, the heavens above—"but more so, a language of the earth. Because I am willing to hear everything without reservations, I hear more than, well, you hear, though you are quite tuned in, so to speak. Those who only venture casually into a forest, they come out here and chalk up the sounds to 'nature,' which only skims the surface. There's so much more going on."

This meshed well with my writing, even the minimally researched phenomenological observations we had spoken of previously. Perception as the trigger for the individual but, more so, for even how we see and *hear* things around us.

"We all perceive things in our own singular ways, as shaped by the lives and experiences and knowledge we have gathered, as well as the essences of who we are and of everything around us. What you're implying is that there is so much more to be perceived, if we allow ourselves to be open to the world around us."

"Precisely."

"Thank you, teacher. That said, how did you pull out such a varied and frightening array of animalistic sounds from your own voice? I mean, how much have you manipulated these recordings?"

She laughed. "This is the raw recording, Derek; minor editing for shape, giving the songs direction, maybe tweak the volume here and there." I'd picked up on that much. There had to be more. "Mostly I just let them form of their own accord. I have done nothing of real manipulation as of yet." She got up, took my mug along with hers, and went to the kitchen to fill them up again.

I had to explore further. There was no way I could picture the pure feral vibrancy of the vocals I had just heard. Sure, this was far out and thought provoking, as was all of her inspiration and knowledge about sounds, but that was her job as well as the focus of her life's interests. She's a musician, she has utilized so much more than I could imagine in the shaping of herself as a musician, especially within that which she even perceived as music.

"I know you are a talented and eclectic musician and singer. That much I have gleaned from your work with Dark Angel Asylum and the solo CDs. But how can you tell me those sounds, the potency of the vocals in such an inhuman cadence, have not been manipulated in some way? I mean, the primal quality of your voice is, dare I say, frightening."

"You know my work. Don't you wonder about the shifting personalities and characters within different songs? A demon in one song, a young girl in another; someone more ancient than imagined in another. I could go on."

"Sure, I thought it was like...have you heard the David Bowie CD, *Outside*? There are a few tracks where he incorporates a different voice, the voices of characters, a nod to the principles of theater, perhaps."

"Bowie was always a chameleon, which is a better way to look at what I've been doing. I'm sure a part of me can't help but to incorporate whatever is necessary, even so much as to include my own theatrical digressions, while the songs take shape, but what I am doing is more like what the field recordings are doing. I am channeling the vibrations that are around us." She opened her palms like a gameshow model, displaying something she really could not display: the mysteries that enveloped us. "Two tracks so far, no language that you would understand, me either, for that sake, but there is a language out there. I'm taking the vibrations and letting them flow through me and expressing them as best as possible."

"Are you saying your vocals are pure improvisation, that there was nothing of forethought before you stepped into the forest?"

"No forethought, but not pure improvisation. I sense, while I am out there, the essences, the characters, for those not willing to believe in the possibilities, and I settle into a trance-like state as I record, and whatever essence is present, whichever essence has the strongest vibration and demands expression, I allow it my larynx to *express* itself. It is language, though one that maybe we, as humans, at least at this stage of our development, or even this stage of our lives, cannot fully comprehend." She caught her breath, almost rapturous in the collision of ideas and seeming pleased with a somewhat perceptive confidante for these declarations. "Look, Derek. There are many possibilities as to what I am having a hand in creating, more so, exploring. I feel that the sounds and the songs I shape from these recordings are more like reflections of the world condensed down to their root element, something crystalline and perfect, and I am trying to bottle this perfection of sound for dissemination via the music and, hence, the CDs I create. I would do this no matter what, you know."

I decided to see if anything she was experiencing jibed with any of Frank's assumptions. "So if there are possibilities, since there *are* possibilities, couldn't what you're tapping into awaken or attract negative forces within nature as well?"

"Of course that is a possibility. But I like to think that positive forces outweigh negative forces or, at least, because of the person I am, with my mindset geared toward something positive, that I am immune, I suppose, to that which is negative, and allowed to explore freely."

With my present experience, I almost thought this naïve, but did not say it out loud. Then again, with her experiences with Dark Angel Asylum, Aleister Blut and all that, I was sure she was aware of the possible naivety of the statement and had moved beyond the potential reception of negative influences and into the realm of pure creativity without fear.

Nonetheless, this time I let Lovecraft slip out, saying, "'The most merciful thing in the world...is the inability of the human mind to correlate all its contents.'"

"But what of the world itself? The most merciful thing might not be just the inability of the human mind to correlate all its contents, but all of that which surrounds it as well. This world, nature, the universe. Everything. Though curiosity is a driving force for most people, this inability to correlate *everything* might be our saving grace. Merciful, as Lovecraft suggests."

I was surprised by her somber shift in perception, moving away from the purely positive, as if she understood the breadth of possibilities. No, she wasn't naïve.

"Must be why curiosity kills cats," I said, leavening the conversation, my attempt to come up for air.

"Must be why cats are given nine lives," Alethea said, the corners of her lips curling up.

"I envy your complete freedom, Alethea."

She meowed. We laughed.

Our joviality was broken as we heard a car screech into Frank's driveway. We got up and headed to a window. A figure stood next to the driver's side door, shutting it.

Izzy.

I did not want to leave but knew the circumstances demanded my participation at Frank's house. This was too compelling to leave up in the air for long.

"I truly hate to cut this short, but that's Izzy, and he's part of the reason I'm up here."

"You must come over again, tomorrow if possible." Alethea said this while staring at Izzy as he stood next to the car and stretched. There seemed something of suspicion or, at the least, a keen awareness in her eyes. I got the impression that what we were doing while I was listening to the field recordings, what I was learning, had a purpose beyond the guise of listening to music and sounds and talking about the inspirations behind them.

Was she just opening up avenues for character development, or was she showing me something more important about her, or even about the world around me? And, more specifically, the world around me here, at Frank's place?

I was curious, for sure, and wary of overanalyzing everything. Why would there be anything deeper to show me? If there was, why wouldn't she just say so? Why was I shaping something out of nothing, reading suspicion in her look when I am sure there was no substance behind it? Frank's mood had messed with my already over-analytical thought processes. I wouldn't be surprised if there was steam coming out of my ears.

"You know I will. Might be a couple days, not sure. I mean" — I turned to her, pulling her focus from Izzy to me, letting her know where I was coming from—"I don't want to forestall what is in motion, what with your music and…stuff."

"Stuff," she said, and kissed my cheek. "Don't take too long, Derek. Time is of the essence."

With the kiss, I knew she understood. With the remark, she added another ingredient to the kettle of vague allusions that Frank and even being here had filled, now brimming over the top.

12: Dizzy Izzy

As I passed by Izzy's car, something generic that looked like a bar of soap, and missing a license plate as well, he turned and saw me. Years ago I would have made a blatant bad remark, something perverse and squeezed between the jiggling cheeks of disgust. Something very Izzy-like. But now, with the letter, I didn't know what to expect from him, so I waited for him to make the first move.

"Derek?" Recognition. "Derek!"

His face glowed. He looked barely older than when I'd last seen him, his features still etched with the childlike glee that always made whatever he did a joy to witness because it fairly bubbled out of his face. A face that was so average, as Frank would say, when not immersed in comedy.

He ran toward me and gave me a bear hug, lifting me up. I did the same in return, some kind of macho bonding ritual in motion.

He seemed fine, absolutely himself.

"Did you ever get that 'Enter Here, Big Boy' tattoo removed from your ass, Derek?"

He *was* completely fine, in a manner of speaking.

"It's been too long, Izzy. My, you look well-preserved."

"Pickle juice facials and being massaged by elderly Japanese men to keep the muscles supple will do that for you," he said, hand still clenching mine.

I had so much to say, yet it tumbled out awkwardly. "You were everywhere, then not. Kind of like what happened with Dave Chappelle."

"Yeah, Dave and me, we're tight."

"Then, with the letter..." I stopped, not sure how to go about expressing my concern over the letter to Frank.

"What letter?"

He looked at me, goofy wide grin and absolutely no idea what I was talking about.

"The one you sent to Frank. The one with the foreboding message and signed Isadora—"

"Whoa, Nellie. Isadora? You know the sentence to those who call me Isadora. Drop trou, grab your ankles, and call in the natives—"

"What? You didn't sign it Isadora, with a lower case 'i' as well?"

"Dude, I haven't sent any letter."

"What the fuck?" Complete confusion. "Why are you here?"

"Because I miss you dudes."

"Really, Izzy? We've not heard from you in eight years and here you show up, out of the blue."

"Look. I'm back in the states after eight years in Germany, married and loved it, but at some point I needed to get back in touch with myself and she needed to take care of her own demons, so we did the amicable split deal and here I am. Lock up your daughters, America, Dizzy Izzy is back!"

"Just like that, eight years and out?"

"Well, yes." He calmed down, the memories simmered. "We're still in touch, but we knew a couple years ago that the best of what we had was in the past and in order not to just grow to hate each other, breaking up was necessary. And, as I said, the performance itch started coming on strong. I thought it was gone, maybe I thought love had conquered it, but a part of me I thought was buried decided to unearth itself and I found myself writing some material, a screenplay. It was inevitable."

"If you didn't write a letter to Frank, why are you here?"

Again with his puppy dog eyes: "Because I miss you dudes, Derek."

I had to smile, the guy was a goof.

"C'mon, wiener. The truth, tell me the truth."

"Did I ever tell you the one about the famous writer who lost his marbles, only to realize they weren't his marbles in the first place?"

"What the fuck is that supposed to mean?"

Izzy smiled slyly, as if he had a secret. I wasn't smiling. It wasn't funny. Under the circumstances it was rather discomfiting.

"It's not like it took much to track you dudes down." Back to normal, or at least some semblance of normal, erasing the unexpected aside. "You're both popular, y'know? And since I'm staying in Seattle, the calm before the Dizzy Izzy comeback storm, stoking interest again in a more civilized city than Hollywood, the drive down to Los Angeles hits Frank's humble abode first. I just lucked out that you were here, too."

I had to think, though: Why was I here? If Izzy hadn't written a letter, why had Frank called me here in the first place? *Who had written the letter?* Had Frank, by God, written the letter, a kind of plea for help? And what were the chances that Izzy would show up out of the blue, as Frank had said he would, if he *hadn't* written the letter? My brain ached and I needed an aspirin or three, maybe something to chase them down that burned with purpose.

"Let's find out what's going on," I said, heading for the door, knowing I would wake Frank up if he was sleeping, but banking on him being wide awake.

Izzy bellowed, "Lucy, I'm home," as we entered.

The place was eerily silent.

"Frank. Hey, Frank," I said.

Nothing.

I started up the stairs. When I made it to Frank's room, he was nowhere to be found. Back downstairs, I flicked the switch on for a merry-go-round rimmed lamp. Pale stallions and multi-colored beasts frolicked around the lampshade. I noticed a note taped to the television screen. "Gone fishing."

I was at a loss, and noticed that the writing was much as the writing in the alleged note written by Izzy. You'd think knowing Frank all these years I would recognize his handwriting, but with technology and email and such, I honestly couldn't say I'd seen anything he had handwritten in years, as if it really would matter, until now.

I peered out the window, to the forest, and said, "He can't be long," more for my reassurance than because it was something I actually believed.

Frank had been "gone" my whole time here. How was I to know how much longer he would be gone, and on what level, the mental or the physical, he would be gone?

I also wondered what he was fishing for this time.

"Lovely place, five star amenities. Who's Frank's realtor—Lincoln? Probably had that Bunyan dude build this place. I hear he works on the cheap for blue body paint and coonskin hats, has a fetish for oxen," Izzy said, as he perused the disheveled interior.

I smirked, amused with Izzy's riffing, but uncomfortable with the turn of events. Everything seemed out of sorts here, except maybe the time I had spent with Alethea. Even Izzy seemed odd—time will do that—but what had time done to him? The oddness I was picking up from him was more because of how much he hadn't changed. He seemed exactly as he had been before, well-preserved, indeed.

"Does he do these late night fishing trips often?"

"Not since I've been here, but I've only been here a few days. We actually ventured out that way yesterday, but Frank changed his mind, so we didn't make it all the way to the river." What was I to say? I hadn't seen Izzy in eight years, why lay something this undefined on him, yet. "He's remarked that it helps him get his brain straight, but considering he's barely left the house since I got here…" Again, I had to stop. Trying to explain Frank's present condition was beyond my skills as a wordsmith. I wasn't even going to bring up the restaurant debacle from today.

"Whatcha got to drink here?" Izzy wandered toward the kitchen, checking the refrigerator before opening cabinets.

"Top one. To the left." I knew what he wanted and figured that a slug of something to chase down the aspirin was in the cards.

He pulled down a bottle of Jack Daniels, no messing about, let's get down to it. I pulled down two glasses, not shot glasses but, anyway, I had the impression we would be drinking more than a measly shot this late evening. I eagerly relinquished any aspirations for health or even keeping my head straight.

I pinched and twisted the cap off a bottle of aspirin I'd pulled down from the cabinet next to the one with glasses, and shook out two pills.

We sat in the dim light. One of the bulbs was out, though we had no inclination to change it at this time. Izzy filled our glasses and didn't hesitate to tilt his head back sharply and drain his. I chased the aspirin with my own big swig.

Izzy coughed, let out an, "Ah, *yeah*! That's more like it," in appreciation of the alcohol, and said, "Now, tell me what's up with you dudes, Derek."

I stared back at him, the burn still singeing my esophagus. I shook my head at the atypical turn of events with Frank since I'd arrived. Nothing seemed to be fully formed, his distracted mind blurring everything for me as well. I had no idea what really was up with him, though the possibility of the need for psychiatric help seemed an option, yet beyond that kind of thinking, I was worried. Frank's mind seemed on the steep downslope toward a breakdown, for sure.

"If I really knew what was up I could answer that, Izzy. I mean, besides the writing, which is what we do, not much to say."

I didn't feel like going over our histories since we'd last seen him. I felt he probably knew of the novels and expected diversions on some level. He was there for some of ours and we were there for much of his, until he left. What I felt was more pertinent was dealing with the here and now. "Frank sent me an urgent email, requesting I come up for a bit. Said he wanted me to help him deal with stuff. I figured he was in a partying mood and since I was between projects, I figured it was good timing. But when I got here, he showed me a letter he said you sent him. We've already gone over that, which pretty much catches you up; that's where everything stands."

I had to let it gel, still waiting to see what developed.

"Christ, I haven't seen you in years. Give me details about the reemergence of Dizzy Izzy."

"Not a whole lot to add to what little I already said. I was married. I got the comedy itch again, about two years ago, got to writing new material, a screenplay that puts my others to shame, and new stand-up material, demented stuff that had me laughing out loud."

"I still don't get how you could stop cold turkey in the first place."

"Love, amigo. It was love. You know me, nothing special to look at, all personality, but being in the biz, most of the women I attracted were of the groupie ilk. They want to be with me for a night, maybe a week or two, latch onto a piece of stardom, whatever the motivation. Me, you know I like that, probably as much a part of the reason I got the itch again since my love with Jesse, since *our* love, had petered out." He rubbed two fingers together next to his ear, as if playing a miniature violin. Oh, the tragedy! It seemed rather heartless to me. "When I met Jesse, it was different. She barely knew of my work but liked my sense of humor outside of that, as well as other stuff that pretty much let me know if I was ever gonna give marriage a shot, she was the one to do it with. Anyway, love was good, but now it's done. I think for me the desire to perform again became so strong that I couldn't deny it, and that desire goes hand in hand with the desire to meet my fans again."

"Rock star perks even on the comedy circuit, eh?"

"Old school rock star perks. You know how crazy this all can get. All fun, but after a while, even that wears you down. But at this time in my life, I need that madness again, to leap into the fray and roll with the punch-lines, see if I still got it, which, trust me, as I just said, the new stuff puts the old stuff to shame."

"Is it like the old material or have you, God forbid, matured?"

I was glad to be relaxing, the drink flowing through me, massaging muscles from the inside, the conversation a welcome distraction from the discomfort that slinked through the back of my brain. I looked out the window, not really expecting to see Frank. My head was starting to get foggy, but I took another swig and listened as Izzy, seeming none the worse for wear, continued.

"I've got a different perspective, maybe. It is different. I think it still sounds like me, but there's a more surreal quality to it. My former stuff was surreal, but in a crude way. Now what I write, I'd say the screenplay is more like something Lynch would do, if he ever did pure comedy."

"Sounds good," I said, eyelids growing heavy. "Can't wait to read it, see the movie."

"It is good. Very good. Y'know, Derek, perspective is a key to so many things in this world." His tone had shifted. He sounded like a TV pitchman, hawking something intangible that I already had a wealth of, yet still insisting I could use some of what he brought to the table. "Like, what's up with Frank? What's he really need from you anyway, eh?"

My eyes throbbed, a sensation that skewed my vision. Izzy's head seemed to swell and deflate. I remembered acid trips I'd experienced with Frank in college, only a few. This felt much like that.

The walls glistened as snail trails, the busy black corner at the far end of the room indicative of their orgiastic destination, though I could not see for sure and did not want to confirm this perception.

The walls throbbed as well, the knots imbued with a gentle flexibility that hinted at breathing. I heard sounds like voices, but not voices, not *exactly*.

"Have another, Derek," Izzy said, pouring me more Jack Daniels, swigging from the bottle and setting it next to a couple more bottles. When had he gotten those down?

Something thick squirmed in the tight confines of one of the bottles. It stared back at me with one large, penetrating eye. As if it could see into my brain and read my thoughts.

"What the..." slipped past my lips, less an incomplete thought and more a smeared ink stain, my thoughts buckling down into a kind of sudden hypnagogic limbo.

My brain ached with the intrusion, something I distinctly felt. As if beetles were treading over it, or picking at it, the tiny pinch of their sharp-angled exoskeletons and legs tipped with claws making me spasm.

I heard Izzy say, "Derek another, have," though his mouth didn't move.

A sibilant sound slithered from the wooden walls. Knots flexed and hissed at me.

"What the fuck is going on?" I said, or thought, but it didn't matter, it was relayed and understood. Izzy smiled, his teeth mustard yellow and rubbery as they squished together. A clown's exaggerated leer.

I blinked, felt the function deep in my body, as if the process had been something the body felt necessary to participate in, fearing I couldn't do it without the assistance.

When I opened my eyes, Izzy was gone.

I stood and teetered, grabbed the edge of the table and sat back down, calling out, "Derek," and laughing to myself for my idiocy. I am Derek. I am so fucking drunk. How did this happen so fast? Is this the analytical brainslush that usually fills my head when alcohol takes over? Or is this the analytical brainslush that usually fills my head, whether alcohol is present or not?

"Izzy," I said, mesmerized as the elasticity of the knots mocked mouths. Words registered in my head, not that I heard them with my ears.

"I'm right here, where Frank wants me to be, dude."

Izzy's voice swam in my head, but I still couldn't see him. Where was he?

"I'm right here. Open your eyes, dude. Focus. Open your eyes."

"My eyes are open," I said, recoiling, as the beetles that picked at my brain made their presence known, pouring out of the mouths in the wood where the knots used to be, vomited with force like bats from a cave at dusk. I tried to get up, but the muscles in my legs had turned liquid, the bones seemed to bend at unusual angles, a daisy-chain of disobedient joints but, anyway, my brain was uncooperative, the messages intercepted and laughed at by neurons on hiatus—let us be, let us be, savor the beetle spectacle!

The beetles continued to pour out of the cavern-like mouths, still hissing—the mouths or the beetles, I wasn't sure—a relentless onslaught.

The busy black corner grew pregnant, distended as a dark cloud about to burst.

My breath screamed in my ears, a sound like something tearing, fabric threaded with metal, pulled apart by the strong hands of a giant baby, a clumsy colossus. The sound of everything being ripped apart without care, ripped for the sheer satisfaction of the noise it inspired.

13: Reality, Slipping...

"Help me, Izzy."

I said this to the empty kitchen, forcing myself to rise again. None of this was real, it couldn't be, but why was this more like a caustic acid trip than the lazy drift of drunkenness? Where was Izzy? The bathroom, perhaps, or perhaps he'd stepped outside, maybe this or that, but please, "Let me see you again—"

You'll see me again when it's the proper time, dude, a voice said, not Izzy's voice, this one weary as hammered metal. Personality, something Izzy towed by the trailer full, was unlatched and empty. Something in it reminded me of what I'd always thought Average Joe's voice would sound like in his more contemplative moods. Most of the time it was described as a monotone drone, but Frank wrote his dialogue as a more insidious, in your face spin on Freddy Krueger. "True deadspeak," he called it, as if he really understood the blunted nuances.

I was feeling the same way the contact high had made me feel at Izzy's birthday bash: uncomfortable in my own skin. It reminded me of the many concerts Frank and I had seen featuring the eclectic metal band, Raptor Elegance, and their vocalist, Skrich, more insect than human; an insect trying to escape from the prison of flesh it was wrapped in. It was as if I had a peripheral sniff of something, perhaps the past, as intruded upon by the strange present here at Frank's place.

Or was this an actual acid flashback, though we had only done acid a handful of times? Maybe a few times too many...

The walls were covered with beetles, the knots that were mouths were now dark pits that housed broken mustard yellow teeth, as if they had been kissed by a fist. This predicament was only temporary, as the mouths mutated into something else.

Eyes.

Mouths puckered and closed, and with each re-opening, bloodshot and glazed eyes stared at me while beetles scrambled over the glossy lenses; the trespass was negligible, their focus, unwavering.

Christ, I wished my body would function again, my shaky status hindering the need to run, or at least crawl out the damned door; crawl like a beetle.

Leaning on the wood stove, I glanced down and the letters— the letters were completely different now, tiny and stretched across the front. It said, "Almost time, dude."

All around me sounds buzzed and chattered. All around me leaves rustled. I was sticky hot to the point of physically feeling feverish.

Something was more than amiss. It was hungry in ways I did not want to understand.

"Izzy," I said, knowing he wasn't going to respond, at least not in the flesh.

Frank's laughter pressed into my thoughts.

Everything seemed to stagger to a sludgy slowdown and my head felt like it was full of helium.

I peered out to the forest, wobbling as I stood, my balance precarious, my hand away from the oblique message of the wood stove, seeking purchase on the table again.

I saw a face in the darkness, then just darkness.

The most powerful sensation I felt was that this was what it felt like in Frank's head right now, all mush, confusion, a sense of paranoia on a personal level, as if something—

The face again...or not? My eyes were mutinous in their scrutiny of the ever-shifting *everything*.

It felt like insanity, and knowing this was insanity, and from my perspective, knowing that everything I was sensing was Frank's insanity, somehow (telekinetically? why not?) showing me something that I refused to acknowledge at this time, though it was making headway, I'd give it that much.

I also understood that the forest heightened everything I was feeling, and, as a matter of fact, might be the ringmaster for these revelations. Again, as Frank had suggested.

Either that or I was going insane as well.

Something else in my ears, nibbling at my attempts to analyze what was in motion: more laughter, but not Frank's this time, not exactly. It was like a mirror, this laughter, like a mirror into Frank's mind, and it let me hear a laughter that could only be the laughter of his most famous creation, Average Joe—"...dry as dust awakened, his laugh raised goose bumps and dread alike, the sound of shadows conspiring to steal one's life, the sound of the murderer, no conscience, no soul."

Average Joe, a fictional character, was getting a lot of screen time on the cranial cinema within my skull, soundtrack included. Even if he lurked in the shadows, beyond confirmation, I knew he was there.

I glanced to the bottles, an array of green and deep brown, of clear and burgundy, all of them now filled with meaty things that struggled against the glass and stared at me.

Much like the walls.

I moaned again, this time a prayer released—"Please, God"—whether I believed or not, the circumstances breaking me down a little more with every passing second.

I heard that sound again, the most perfectly sinister sound I have ever heard in my life; it was most definitely not human, that laughter.

I felt everything spin, my breath exhaled with force as if being hit in the stomach with a baseball bat, and tumbled down a staircase within my skull, a long stretch between conception and cessation, before landing as a sack of bones at the bottom, broken beyond repair. Abandoned by all the king's horses and all the king's men.

I was in the forest again, wandering, enveloped in a hive of voices, indistinguishable amidst the clutter, but voices, so many voices.

Then:

"Wake him up."

"No, he hasn't been sleeping well. Let him sleep."

"You haven't slept worth shit yourself, eh?"

"We haven't slept worth shit."

A rustle of paper, a flutter of insect wings: laughter.

"Leave a note."

"You write it."

"No, you write it."

A "ping" like razor-wire being stretched taut and plucked: a trap being set.

"Does it matter who writes it?"

"Nah. He won't be able to tell the difference."

"Hasn't so far, has he?"

"Maybe, but it only adds to the fun, don'tcha think?"

"Fun?"

The paper crackles now, as if set on fire: laughter, in stereo.

"Sure you don't want to wake him up?"

"He'll wake up soon enough. He'll wake up soon enough."

"Yeah, I suppose. It's time for him to wake up anyway."

"Now!"

I gasped, words racing for relief, "Frank. Izzy. Guys..."

I choked and coughed, saliva crust cracking on my tongue, my throat. A thought that the dream and its voices were channeled through my larynx crowded all other thoughts out except one: the voices were identical, no variation. A conversation within my head between what I understood to be Frank and Izzy, or was it Average Joe? Yes, it seemed more like it was Average Joe *and the voices were identical.*

I stood up, tottered, as if my body was an unaccustomed thing, as if this body was not something that I understood the mechanics of anymore. I felt bloated, disorientated.

I scanned the interior of the house though my vision was somehow off as well.

The day seeped in, but the night had left such a deep impact, Izzy here, and alcohol, and everything else.

"Fuckin' lunatic." A familiar voice, that distinct nasal whine whittled to a serrated point, scraped off the walls of my memories as one would scrape dog excrement off one's shoe: Asia.

"What?" I said, swift to turn and face an empty room, no sign of Asia. As if I really expected to see her there.

What I did see was a note taped to the front of the television. As I reached for it I saw my reflection in the dead screen or, rather, I saw Frank's reflection.

I turned again, this time to face a figure I expected to be here, but he was nowhere to be found. The room was empty.

Back to the note, glancing at the screen, it was me now, only my reflection.

I curled my brow as I read the note. It didn't give me information as to their whereabouts. It was a joke, a riddle.

"Did I ever tell you the one about the famous writer who lost his marbles, only to realize they weren't his marbles in the first place, weren't his marbles in the first place, weren't his marbles, weren't his..." On and on, Izzy's failed attempt at humor from earlier, clipped and ragged, now a foreboding signpost on my way to what, or where, or possibly even why.

The sentence, the question, repeated over and over on both sides of the paper. I read every one, and again, looking for something more, flipping the page over and back, then, one sentence:

"Don't you think it's about time you woke up, Derek?"

* * *

Pounding on the door, a female voice, "You okay? Derek, you okay?"

My eyes opened to the gloom of the house, accentuated by heat and tinted with trepidation.

I touched myself, felt my body and knew it was my body. There was no mistaking of this. I didn't know why I did it, but it felt good to confirm this much.

"Derek, you okay?"

Alethea was at the door. I cleared my throat. "Yeah, just a sec. Yeah."

I was adorned in the same clothes as yesterday, having nodded off waiting for Frank—and where was Izzy? Actually, it seemed more likely I had passed out and been escorted to the strangest dreams I'd had up here yet.

I wasn't sure if they were here. I wasn't sure of anything.

I stood and the muscles in my thighs clenched. It felt good. This was real. This was me. It seemed necessary to confirm this.

Something faded as I made my way to the door. The dream, something with voices and messages that made no sense, faded as I opened the door.

"Alethea."

She nudged past me into the house, her eyes taking in the disarray.

"What's up? Why are you here?"

I noticed as her eyes took it all in, and she paused for an extra second on the wood stove.

"I think I was dreaming," I said.

"I suppose that's what you were doing."

What kind of response was that?

"Hey, talk to me. What's going on?"

She turned to me, staring hard, as if reading the lines, maybe between them as I had wanted to do in my dreams.

"Remember last night, my music, my take on vibrations?"

"Sure. It was a place I expected to explore deeper with you."

"I sensed the vibrations of this place were in turmoil."

"This place. Frank's house?"

"This place," she said, still staring into my face, my eyes now, so intense I had to divert them in order to regain some kind of foothold in reality. She was looking too deep into me, as if she were frolicking in my body, my soul, my mind, yes, my mind, and she was taking it all in within me, within this mind, and somehow understanding it, understanding *my* turmoil as well.

A player on the outside, playing on the inside.

Was I still dreaming?

"Fuckin' lunatic." Her lips did not move. It was not her voice. But I knew I heard those words again. The last words Asia had said to me, a pet name turned caustic toward the end of our relationship. As if she had room to speak.

What's that bad expression?—call a spade a spade.

"This place," she said again, her left hand slowly ascending toward my head. I leaned away then stopped. It wasn't as if her intent was to hit me.

She tapped the side of my head.

* * *

I woke up again, this time alone in the room, a thought of being trapped in a *Twilight Zone* gone fucked up version of *Groundhog Day* flitting through my head.

"Fuck. Fuck. *Fuck.*" I leaped off the sofa, having apparently made it to the sofa and fallen asleep or passed out, waiting for Frank and wondering where Izzy was, to no avail.

My clothes clung to me, sweat having pasted them to my flesh. I yelled out, "Frank. Izzy. Guys." No response.

I was up and taking it all in, the house, the landscape outside, noting that Alethea's car was not in her driveway. Veering to my right, I noticed that Izzy's car was also not in the driveway behind my car.

I let out a heavy sigh, something thick with frustration and confusion.

I glanced at the LED clock on the DVD player.

4:33.

I looked outside and thought, *no way. It's got to be at least—*

—then it hit me. 4:33 *in the afternoon.* I'd slept for something like fifteen, sixteen hours.

Everything was out of sync. *Everything*!

I had too many questions racing full throttle in my head, but was distracted as I glanced at the wood stove.

"Bradford." I said it out loud, my fingers tracing the letters. *All of them.*

I was not enjoying this game.

I figured it was time for me to wake up.

14: Absurdity, Alive and Kicking

Phone calls followed, one to Frank, no hesitation in reaching voice mail, indicating he had his cell phone off (as if I could have gotten through anyway), and one to ex-wife number one, Doreen, just wanting to hear a voice that was real. Either hers or, more truthfully, my kids. Something away from this place and the madness that percolated here. Voice mail again.

I glanced out the window toward Alethea's house only to note that her car was still gone.

I took a deep breath and stopped everything. I was not the one in need of any help. My faculties were not suspect. My brain, though veering into some wild, imaginative stuff via the novels, was rooted in the real world.

I understood the real world.

I had responsibilities, paid my bills, said I love you to my kids—sure, most often on the phone, like what I wanted to do just a few minutes ago—wiped my ass like everybody else, brushed my teeth and tried to stay healthy, slipping often. I was just like any other person.

My fiction took the real world and created characters to play in this real world and then set the world on its axis, forcing them to look at everything from a different perspective than they normally would. It was not as far-fetched as Frank's Average Joe series or the Sinister Nature series that followed it. Those stories moved deep into the dark fantastic, the horrific. My stories peeked in on that, but moved on afterwards. I did not wallow there. I did not make the madness my home.

Not like Frank.

Frank's house, this place, seemingly in flux—vibrations misaligned, one might say; *Alethea* might say—only now without anyone here but me, taking shape as substantial, the wood stove with its mocking letters, needling me. Frank, man, what a joker, but how had he done that?

Frank's house seemed like a reflection of his mind and the warped imagination that slinked through it, sleazy attire and wearing a toothless grin and swinging open a ripped, dirty velvet overcoat, flashing diamonds caked in mud. Smiling again, and snakes as tongues danced between chapped lips. I shook my head, because Frank's madness seemed to be infecting my sanity.

When he got back, we would have to head this off now, and get him out of here.

What of Izzy?

Stop it!

None of this made any sense. Bad dreams and weird circumstances and observations shaded in grey did not really mean that anything was wrong.

What I had to do was just like in my fiction. Realize that maybe the world had tilted, look at it from this different angle, and figure out what it all meant.

I called Frank again, voicemail again, this time no message left.

I thought of ways to just relax, quit thinking, always one to overanalyze everything. I'd way overslept. Big deal. I needed the rest. Frank was acting odd. He's gone through other kinds of odd spells before, other kinds of "odd" explored. Izzy—who knows? Alethea—I liked her, really liked the person she was.

I smiled at some of this, the rest I set aside. I sat on the sofa, in need of a mental break. I picked up the remote control and turned on the television. An attractively plastic anchorperson, her hair a sprayed stiff, taffy-colored helmet, reported on the news of the day.

I forced myself to watch and took in the madness of the world. No wonder I wrote fiction that tried to put it all in a place where I could deal with it.

Madness overwhelmed everything. How was one to deal with it?

I watched as bad news, worse news, and nonsensical news was

paraded in front of me like some celebration of the bizarre, not really relaxing me, just taking my focus away from everything the last few days had branded on my brain. Even Alethea, for the time being.

Half focused, mind meandering, I was fully drawn to a somewhat familiar image whose weary façade filled the screen. "All I ever wanted was to be normal, average. All I ever wanted was to forget what I had once created. To destroy it."

It was Aleister Blut, a clip from a few years back. I remembered it from a VH-1 special. The anchorperson continued with the story after the clip.

"Alexander Burroughs, better known as Aleister Blut, former leader of the industrial band, Dark Angel Asylum, escaped from Forsythe Asylum in Washington State last night. Two orderlies were found murdered. In blood on the walls, Burroughs had written, chillingly, 'No future here, not yours or mine.' The authorities have no leads as to his whereabouts."

Absurdity had taken center stage.

I flipped channels, looking for more, surprised at the odd tone of the report, the mention of writings in blood on the walls. Did they always reveal that information so swiftly? Had the world become privy to every iota of every incident, as it happened? I was positive I would find photographs of the bloodied message online if I Googled "Aleister Blut." For all I knew, security tapes of the murders had already made it to YouTube.

Everything seemed subject to Absurdity's whim.

Since the group had disbanded, Aleister Blut has been nothing more than a shadow, a casualty of the madness that he had promoted during the deterioration of Dark Angel Asylum. His ultra-serious demeanor, despite the fact that he used an almost comical, horror-based moniker, which really surprised me the more I had learned about him, had crumbled during that last tour, stage antics gone awry. He often ended up slumped unmoving on the stage for long spells while the band played on.

He'd lost touch with the vital force that had initiated his early career rise, plummeting as a meteor, mentally disintegrating along the way.

The lazy made comparisons to Pink Floyd's Syd Barrett, though Barrett's mental decline was also accentuated by drug misuse. Aleister seemed more cut out of the same cloth as Kurt Cobain or Chelsea Starling, creative individuals who only really wanted to create, and be damned with the games one had to play for the media. The "real" world (a definition that the last few days had seriously thrown out of kilter) something beyond their command.

With his statement, about wanting to be normal and average, it seemed more likely that his mental status was driven less by madness, more by unfulfilled needs, which had led to a kind of madness.

I glanced again toward Alethea's house, silently wishing her car would be in the driveway, wondering if she knew about Aleister's escape, yet somehow suspecting she did, whether she had actually heard the news or not.

Even giving myself a break from the rollicking thoughts in my head, the news only added more to the mix. All I could do at this point was wait, though patience had left the building, with Elvis and quite possibly my sanity. How else to explain last night?

C'mon somebody!

Just as suddenly, my wishes were answered.

"Finally joining the real world, eh? Thought I heard you up."

Shocked, I turned toward the stairs as Frank lumbered down, half smile and a half empty bottle of rum in his hand.

"What the fuck? You've been here all this time?"

He paused, eyes narrowing: "I live here," he said, his expression laced with the unspoken thread of "as if."

"I thought you and Izzy had headed to Boone, or at least somewhere, though I know after our trek yesterday the irrationality of that statement."

Frank raised an eyebrow. "Izzy's here?"

I remembered the note, the reason I'd even thought they had gone anywhere, then remembered the sequence of events and realized that any note written by Frank or Izzy was a product of my dreamstate imagination. This morning, this day moving swiftly to night, had been full, even if spent mostly beneath shuttered eyelids.

"Last night, when you went fishing, he showed up. We waited for you to get back, drank too much."

"I went fishing. I caught nothing. I came back. You were asleep. I stayed awake until dawn. I fell asleep. I woke up by noon. I've actually been constructive since then, locked away in the writing room and writing, fercrissakes. I never saw Izzy."

Impossible.

"When you came in after fishing, didn't you see the car out front?"

"I can't say I was looking out front to notice any car."

I was completely, one-hundred percent miffed, though miffed moved aside as I remembered Frank's "Gone fishing" note from last night, an actual note and not something manufactured by dreams gone loony. At least I thought so...

"Let me see the note Izzy sent you."

Frank ambled to his jacket, took it off the banister where he'd draped it, reached into the inside pocket, pulled out the note, and handed it to me. I grabbed his "Gone fishing" note from the arm of the sofa where I'd apparently stuck it after I'd peeled it off the TV screen, and showed it to Frank.

"Notice anything funny about it?"

"Can't say that I do."

"It looks just like your writing, Frank. This is not funny anymore. Just like the name across the wood stove is not funny, either. Might have been amusing for a second, but now I'm a bit peeved. I want to know what's up."

Frank glanced at the writing. "Looks as much like your writing as it does mine."

"This is not a fucking game. What the hell. Why'd you call me up here in the first place, Frank? And don't tell me some freaky story about Izzy on his way and some phony, cryptic note or this Goddamn forest with a mind of its own crap. Tell me the truth."

In his best Jack Nicholson, he said, "You can't handle the truth!"

"Enough of this shit." I grabbed him by the shoulders. It took every ounce of restraint not to slug him.

He glanced at my hands on his shoulders. I released the grip.

Alethea saw Izzy, I thought. I could at least verify that he was even here when she got back.

Frank held out the rum. I gulped a mouthful without hesitation. Not after last night.

"Aren't you going to ask me about the writing?"

"Why not?" I shrugged my shoulders and plopped down on the sofa.

"I was inspired by something you do with your writing, adding a character into the latest novel culled from real life. From the real world, I mean. Who's to say anything about 'real life'?" He laughed. "Or even the 'real world,' for that matter."

I turned my focus to him. He seemed more himself right now than the whole time I'd been here, at least more the wired, creative side of Frank Harlan Marshall.

"I heard on the news, about that vocalist from the band that Alethea used to be in. Heard about his having murdered the orderlies and escaped from the asylum. I did some research on him and somehow constructed a dual personality for Average Joe—"

"Average Joe?"

"Yeah, he's making a comeback. I just needed a body to infiltrate in order to facilitate Average Joe's resurrection."

"So you have created a crazed rock star to be Average Joe's very own pod person?"

"Well, specifics are still taking shape. I know there's a character that's loosely drawn from Aleister Blut, and the spirit of Average Joe will somehow inhabit this person's body and mind and, well, shit will go bad, as usual in my stuff." He laughed again, this time followed by a swig of rum.

With all sincerity, I said, "I am not enjoying my stay here, Pancho. Not at all."

"Well," he said, shaking the now empty bottle in his hand, "it won't be long, I'm sure."

"Long for what?"

A long pause and a flicker of life in Frank's eyes: "Before we eat some more bad burgers and fries. Let's go, I'm famished."

Oh, that's all, I thought. No deeper meanings. I was the one who would need a vacation after all of this played out, whatever "this" was.

"What about Izzy?"

"Look, you don't gotta believe anything I've said. There was a note, he's on his way, or, as you say, he was here, so I expect he will be back sooner than later, eh?" His hand on my shoulder was not soothing.

I was more than famished. Food might be a good idea. Even bland burgers.

Anything to get out of the house for a bit, to get out and see other people, smell the overdone buns in the restaurant, take in the landscape as we walked, the whole deal. Funny, I felt like so much had come to me in this wasted day, but now none of it made any sense, so what good was it?

I tapped the wood stove. "What about this?"

Frank looked down and said, "Bradford. That's what I thought. How'd you do that?" His smile was different, more open, yet more devious—"a glimmer of joy inspired by the most deceitful designs, happy again in the forest where dreams died and bloodlust was sated." It all came back to Average Joe, it seemed. At least in my head.

15: Pilgrimage

Food was fuel, nothing more. By the time we got back, there was still no sign of Izzy. Where could he be?

Frank excused himself, inspiration dotting his whole conversation over our early dinner, his mind locked into the formation of something that he felt was going to be his best work yet.

Just like that, he seemed more like himself. Maybe it all was a matter of him getting his brain re-wired and rolling properly. I still had to wonder how he would be when Izzy got back, but after my day of warped dreams and the confusion that ran like a rhinoceros through the patchy mental landscape, ramming headfirst into every wily wisp of dreamthought, I was glad he was feeling better, yet still needed to confirm that Izzy's appearance was not a hallucination. Of course, with the Bradford nameplate tomfoolery, hallucinations seemed the order for my stay.

As I stepped out of the shower I heard rubber grind dirt and saw that Alethea had returned. I dressed quickly and headed over.

"How's your friend?"

Just like that I was put at ease. Izzy might be slipping in and out of our lives, but at least I knew that he had been here and it was not some kind of mental degradation in motion. I really wasn't worried about following the path of Syd or Aleister or even Frank, but still…

For all I knew, this really was just some elaborate joke that the two of them had concocted and now it was reaching critical mass.

I could hope so. I'd had enough.

"I'm not really sure. I was actually on the way over here to confirm that you had seen him last night," I said.

"Why wouldn't I have seen him?" She was grabbing bags of groceries out of the back seat of her dark green Prius. She nodded toward the car, a silent request for help.

I picked up the remaining paper bags and followed her inside.

"I hadn't noticed that before," I said, my gaze to the left of the kitchen, where a gym was set up, some fancy machines, an elliptical bike, and various dumbbells.

"Girl's gotta stay fit," she said, flexing her muscle; an impressive muscle, indeed.

"I guess I won't be arm wrestling you, the results might damage my already frayed ego."

I set the bags on the counter and she took out the food. Fruit, vegetables, yogurt, organic juices, and a couple steaks finished off the one bag, much to my surprise.

"I pictured you as a vegetarian, maybe even a vegan," I said, holding up the steaks. She took them from my hand.

"I try to eat healthy, but I'm also realistic. The carnivore side of being human should not be ignored. Occasional meat feeds that part of us that has been with us the longest."

We finished putting her groceries away, no more surprises, and she said, "So, you seemed to walk with urgency on your way over here. What's up?"

I liked her. Get to the point, man!

"I was...I've had a most odd day. Slept through much of it, then nobody was home when I woke up, but eventually I found out Frank *was* home. My brain seemed to lose focus, crazy dreams and such, as if everything that's happened since I'd arrived was piling up and cluttering my thoughts, filling me with not just a splinter but a whole plank of unease." I wasn't sure I was making sense.

"Maybe we should discuss the removal of this plank," she said, brandishing some tongs she had sitting next to the sink. "Have you eaten? I could put those steaks on and grill them to mouth-watering perfection. I'm actually an excellent cook as well as a wonderful conversationalist and easy on the eyes." She smiled, that playful side she'd casually flaunted sneaking out, very much at ease.

I knew she was feeling what I was feeling, the connection

solidifying.

"I wish I hadn't just had the most astonishingly fantastic burgers and home fries up at Skunks."

"Poor you. I don't know how you can eat at that place."

I sensed my brain and body relaxing, all the weirdness that I'd felt over at Frank's house backing into the shadows, more so, bulldozed by the presence of this woman, and my need for something rational to hold on to.

"Yeah, I'm thinking that's the last time I torture my stomach with such high class cuisine."

The night was, as usual, coming on fast. It amazed me how it took no time to go from day to night, barely acknowledging eve, where in San Francisco, time lingered between each, never in a hurry. I wondered what the hurry was up here, and smiled to myself.

"Something funny?" She signaled me to follow her into the big entertainment room.

"Not really. Life is just so different up here."

"Tell me about it. I used to spend most of my time in my other home in New Orleans, one I'd gotten through an inheritance. After Katrina, New Orleans hasn't been the same. It's a shame, because if any place has a grasp of magic, New Orleans is that place. Now I spend my time up here, and it also has its own form of magic, though still very undefined. Well," she laughed, "at least that's how it's different for me. How so for you?"

"It's a different world here. I'm used to city life, not too good at being a nature boy. It's just different." Undefined as the magic here, perhaps.

"Envelop yourself in the magic of it all, I say. Wherever you are." The room brightened measurably as she made her way along the periphery, lighting the many candles as she did.

I hoped to not come off as a jerk by asking, "Do you actually believe in magic?"

She didn't flinch. "I've lived with magic in one form or another all my life. Some things one would not qualify as magic, but I like to look at them as mysterious gifts, so to speak. Signs that magic is in the air."

By this time, I had allowed the sofa to take me into its more than comfortable embrace. "Some things? Like what?"

"Music, for one thing. I look at much of what I have experienced in music and, more so, now that I am taking in the whole of nature, at least as best as I can, as a form of magic. Capturing a moment. Something to be cherished."

"What about performing live, trying to reproduce the same thing over and over. I don't see the magic in that."

She sat in a large leather chair, her focus almost piercing, her abundant jewelry glittering as sunlight on the mottled surface of a pond. "Every moment has its place. I don't do much touring, but when I do, I always try to encompass the acoustics of the venue I am performing in, to feel out its strengths, and to play to those strengths. Same songs, but different ambient textures that influence arrangements, on some level. I appreciate the world I live in and the opportunity to make music, which is what I need to do, for my soul. I know you look at this place, these books"—holding up the *The Phenomenology of Sound*--"and, despite your polite demeanor, think me a bit spaced."

"Quite the contrary."

"I just hope as we get to know each other, you get to know that I am very down to earth and not as crazy as I might seem. I really appreciate your openness to all of this"—broad sweep of her hand, encompassing the whole of the room and all its intricacies, the building blocks for getting to know her better, which would be easy because everything here was something I could relate to in some way, through general interests or novel research—"but you have to understand, after the band broke up, I spent a long time getting to know myself, and for me, this stuff actually means something, even if it's all primarily with a focus for expanding and inspiring my creativity. I just figure you're showing so much interest because you need as much info as you can get for your own creativity, for character development in your next novel."

"It's more than that, Alethea."

She got up from her chair and made her way to the sofa. She sat next to me and took my hand. "I feel *something,* a connection with you that I've not allowed myself to feel for another person in quite some time. But I know creative individuals and know the madness and intensity that is a part of their make-up. There has to be a lack of inhibition in allowing the madness full reign in order to really capture the gist of what one really needs to express creatively. I know how I am. I've known how others are..." Her features seemed to darken: chalkboard memories, once erased, but never permanently forgotten.

I didn't want to break the flow, but her mention of others triggered me into action. "Speaking of others..."

"Ah, yes. Others." She started to rise, but I squeezed her hand and she stayed put.

"You've heard?"

"Yes. I had some email and text messages informing me of Aleister's escape." Her focus centered inward. "His pilgrimage," she said, her smile wry and knowing.

Pilgrimage? What an odd word choice, but I didn't venture its origin or relevance, knowing that there had to be a reason for this word above all others within her take on the situation, and her knowledge of the escapee.

"Do you worry that he might come to see you?"

"I'm sure that's his intention." She looked to our hands, gripping mine tightly. Her features darkened again, a shadow of worry, perhaps.

"You're sure?"

"I knew he had left the asylum before he had left it. Sensed something was amiss that had nothing to do with the usual chaos of life." She paused, focus sketchy, then drawing toward me again, with potency. "I sense things. Always have. You'd think a girl born in New York would be made hard as steel, blocking out the pandemonium inherent to our world, but I've always had a knack for sensing things. Probably why I ended up in New Orleans and now here. Sometimes I sense things before they've happened. Sometimes it's just a feeling that things are off and wondering what I can do to make them right. Sometimes it's just knowing, like with people, that I'm supposed to know a person, straight up, no questions asked, this person is somebody I need to know, like with you."

I found myself putting my arm around her shoulders, wanting to pull her closer, yet she surrendered without my insistence. As she leaned into the crook of my shoulder, her warmth and the gentle pressure of her presence made my flesh tingle.

"Anyway, yes, I sensed it and was not surprised by his having left the asylum."

Before he left the asylum. Another strange choice of words. After all, he'd murdered two orderlies.

"Yes. He did." An outward response to my unspoken thoughts. Shadows grew strong and darkened not just her features but the room; the night had taken hold. Unlike yesterday, the candlelight waned at its approach.

"Did you sense that?"

"If I say yes, are you going to leave?" She sat up, eyes to mine again, searching.

"Of course not."

"Even if I might come off as crazy, though I am obviously—"

"Not. No, you're not crazy. Perceptive in ways that I can only understand from the outside. But crazy? Like you said, you believe in things, or have interest in things, that might send some people away shaking their heads. Me, nah, I've had my share of crazy, especially over the last few days. This isn't crazy. Eclectic maybe; thought-provoking, you bet. But crazy…"

She seemed to take it all in, and added one more thing to her litany of sensory overload.

"Your friend, Frank, has been up here for a while. We'd only exchanged polite head nods up to now."

"I'd wondered why you hadn't actually met until the other day."

"I don't think I'm his type," she said, dimples cutting through again.

"I don't know if Frank even knows what his type is."

"Anyway, recently I've sensed some kind of turmoil in the air, the aura or energy of this place, of"—she licked her lips, lightly sighed—"his place."

"Well, he is a bit off. Writer's block and such, though today he said he started to crawl out of it." As if his writer's block might be why she was sensing turmoil.

I thought of Frank's mindset and everything he had touched on since my arrival. I also thought of my day, the dreams that distorted everything, and of Alethea tapping my head when speaking of "this place" in one of those dreams from only a few hours ago.

"I don't know what to make of it," she said, as if maybe I had the answers.

"Don't make anything of it, I say. He's just going through a rough spell, though still being a practical joker as well." I couldn't get the wood stove out of my thoughts as I said this, wondering: what was the purpose of it all? I remembered many stories in which one person tried to make another go crazy, but what purpose, what gains, would Frank have in pushing me that way? I knew it was just something he did for his amusement, but still.

But it did make me think everything was slipping into gear, and something more was on the way.

Now I was the perceptive one.

"We should take a walk in the forest."

Where did that come from? I'm sure I squirmed in my seat.

"Um, well…" I remembered my discomfort the other day, yet didn't want to allow my overactive imagination, as corrupted by Frank's insane input, to deter anything I had developing with Alethea.

"Don't worry, I'll hold your hand. I'll protect you." She placed both hands on mine, squeezing with intent.

There was no doubt we were going to walk in the forest. I just hoped she really had what it took to protect me.

16: The Forest

The darkness was oppressive, as if it were a living thing trying to squeeze the confidence out of me: a boa constrictor, tenderizing the meal.

"You can hold it if you want." She waved the flashlight; rays sliced through the night, glimpses of tree trunk and branch, of brambles and dirt, in swirling disarray. Slivers of forest, it seemed. Snapshots.

"I'd rather hold your hand—"

"*I wanna hold your hand,*" she sang loudly, a jolt that amused me greatly. The words died somewhere above us, at the tops of the trees, maybe eaten by the starry night. The thought made me think of one of Van Gogh's most famous paintings, "Starry Night," and how the night in the painting looked so tumultuous, so alive.

I pulled her closer.

"You want to hold more than my hand, don't you?"

"Are you coming on to me?" I said, even though I'd taken the next step.

The air was humid. She nuzzled into me, breath hot against my neck. Sweat melded us together, the side of my shirt to the side of her blouse.

"Sticky," she said, pulling away only to crowd in closer, as if this place she nuzzled was her place, where she had always belonged.

I wasn't feeling anything weird out here this time. My senses were locked into Alethea, this astonishing woman, and not the miasmal sensations and smells that had assaulted me previously.

"Hey," I said, pulling her face from its half-hearted perusal of the landscape, and my neck.

"Yes, hey," she said, the lids of her eyes dipping slightly.

We kissed, her lips so soft, collapsing at the force of our desire, our tongues entwined as if they had a purpose beyond the simple edicts of a kiss, as if something buried deep within was being awakened and I was not sure if it was love or some primal urge or just confusion fluttering about in my head and body, loins tingling and aroused as well.

I remember being seventeen and the first real kiss I'd ever had—me, a late bloomer—not some spin-the-bottle slobbery mess, but that kiss that lets one know that something more was in motion, and exploring that something more was going to be so much fun. A kiss that feels like it has a life of its own, as if the two lips are taking the lead and the rest of the body and brain better strap in because something new has been discovered. I remember leaving that girl's house (another redhead—my curse) before her parents got home—she was home sick from school, me not even worried about germs or the consequences of cutting school myself— running a bit because of the energy flowing through me, feeling more alive than I'd ever felt before. I remember leaping to grab a leaf off a tree, leaping and feeling like I could fly, like flight was a definite possibility. And why not? I felt superhuman, yet deep down I felt so vulnerable I wanted to cry even as a smile that wouldn't go away for the rest of the day was plastered on my face.

Alethea reluctantly pushed away, a smile as wide as the ocean on her face, the stars that could peer in on us amidst the tall trees adding a twinkle to her eyes. Her eyes, alive, something more than just seeing me, but taking in all of me, devouring me, as I am sure mine were doing to her.

She kissed me again, lighter now, words swift to follow. "I think we should remove these pesky clothes."

My initial thought was, "Here?" but I swatted that away. Of course here! Absolutely, without inhibition or delay here!

I helped her unbutton her blouse. She let it glide to the soft dirt. Her bra was swift to follow. I noticed color peeking over her shoulders, tattoos of vines—green, brown; flowers that introduced a new spectrum of colors to the familiar rainbow panoply—and, despite the fact that she had full, amazing breasts that I wanted to hold against me, maybe forever, I turned her around.

An explosion of design met my eyes, the flashlight now in my hand, my observation one of awe. From mid back to lower back she had a tattoo of the earth, as one would picture it from one of the space flights, though with something more that added depth, something elusive, as if in touching it, the cartography would have texture: moist oceans, ridged mountain ranges. I thought it might seem like more just because of whom the artwork was on, as if her presence added something more, the lean musculature of her wondrous back.

My fingers skated across her shoulders to a crescent moon, the inadvertent chill they inspired raising goose bumps along the way, accentuating the cartographical fleshscape that was the earth below their trespass.

"A crescent moon has many meanings, but it is, as the moon itself is, always in transition, in a constant state of transformation. I like to think that is how I am. You know how I look at formula and such, so that is the major significance, as well as the obvious."

"The obvious?" I said. Though my eyes were focused on the individual tattoos, the undeniable lure of her lovely body drew their attention as well.

"It's a purty tattoo, Billy Bob," she said, in a precise exaggeration of redneck twang. It caught me off guard, amused me to no end. I laughed and continued my exploration.

Thin, delicate yet finely detailed ivy caressed her shoulders, slid down and encircled everything. I could see more of the design peeking from alongside each hip, crawling up from the waist of her jeans.

"There's more," she said, kicking off her sandals and unsnapping her jeans. I set the flashlight on a log, our only company in this empty patch, so that it shined on her, suddenly wondering if this was the same patch where Frank and I had conversed. I tugged on the jeans, helping her step out of them. She wore no underwear.

My breathing grew heavy. The personality had intrigued me so very much, but now, the most exquisite body I had ever laid eyes on was unveiled. Okay, maybe circumstances were enhancing things, but I didn't care in the least. There was a perfection here that could not be blunted by my over-analytical mind.

I followed the ivy down the side of each leg, ending at her ankles.

"Ivy, ivy everywhere," I said.

"You do know the significance of ivy, señor?" The accent was perfection. She seemed in transition at all times. The crescent tattoo seemed most appropriate.

Something buzzed in the back of my brain, rifling through the files, to no avail. Too distracted to pull up the info. But I played it off, "Um, yes. Yes, I do."

"You don't sound too sure of yourself, Derek." Her eyes followed my fingers as they hovered over the twisted path of the ivy. "Fidelity. It stands for many things, as with all symbols, but for me, it's the aspect of fidelity that stands out the most with ivy."

"Fidelity? You're a single woman."

"Ah, the question of fidelity to who or what? Perhaps it's to me and my art. Perhaps it's to a man I had yet to meet when I had the work done, yet he's always been with me, within my soul, a part of my soul, spiritually aligned. It also stands for permanence, which kind of fits as well, if this man has been with me for so long. And now…" Her intimations were clear. She took my hovering fingers and pressed them against her hips. They continued their glide downwards.

"Fascinating," I said, not even sure how I got the word out, what with the sensation of the swoop of her shape making my body ache and my brain buzz. But I was truly fascinated by everything about her and her suggestion, that perhaps this man had always been with her on some spiritual level or more, and now was made flesh, in the real, fascinated me as much as her flesh, and the reality of her.

"It's not fair if you don't share," she said, turning to me. Her thighs clenched, a light dusting of red hair present above her vagina. I could smell her desire, her arousal. A glimmer of moisture winked at me.

I looked up to her and she held out her hand. I forced myself to stand, feeling a bit shaky at the sight of her.

I regained a semblance of composure when I realized she might enjoy my tattoo, too, as well as my obvious arousal.

I took off my shirt.

"I read in an interview that you have a splendid old tree tattoo on your back," she said, turning me around. "Oh, my," she said, her hand caressing the whole of my back, Doreen's artwork delighting another woman. I had to chuckle.

"Am I tickling you?"

"No. Please continue."

It was something to behold, as my ex-wife was a supreme stylist specializing in highlighting the intricate details of her subject matter. Not so much me, but the tree.

"I thought you would like that," I said, relishing her fingers as they traced the tree's outline.

"The tree from *Breathing Shadows*—beautiful. That might still be my favorite novel by you. All the subtle nods to mythology."

"What?" I was dumbfounded, or just dumb.

"Mythology. Another one of my fond friends."

"Let's hope none of your fond friends makes an appearance out here tonight."

"Let's hope not," she said, fingers still tracing the tree, from the mysterious shapes within the shadows, and out to the branches, the leaves.

"Much like the Tree of Life, rooted in our earth, but reaching to the heavens."

Above us, the leaves decided to perk up, rustling without the accompaniment of wind, as if Alethea's caresses had inexplicably projected to them.

"Ohhh, creepy," she said.

"Yeah...creepy," I said, a bit more uneasy about the interruption than she was.

Though Alethea seemed completely taken by the tattoo, she said, "You're not done yet," as she pulled on the waist of my jeans.

"What?" I said, turning to give her a sideways, peek-a-boo smile, shaking my temporary discomfort.

She reached around and unbuckled my belt, unsnapped my

jeans, and pulled hard. She knelt down and plucked my shoes off, then my pants and my underwear, though that took a little adjusting as my erection tied things up, but not for long.

I turned to face her, helping her up. Nothing felt awkward, nothing felt self-conscious.

We moved closer, hands kneading, flesh meshing, lips meeting again, and it all made sense.

This was where I was always meant to be, it seemed. Or at least that thought streaked through my head.

She pulled me to the dirt, having swiftly arranged the clothes into a make-shift sheet, and we lay amidst the dark splendor of the forest, immersed in each other, time inconsequential, me thinking, "I wonder what would be relevant without her in my life," and responding in my head, "Nothing, nothing would matter." But thoughts were on the backburner as pure passion and every other word that thinks itself in relation to passion made our coupling the only thing that mattered in the world. Everything clicked into place, the intellectual, the physical, a visceral psychology melding between us. We were so connected it might inspire anxiety if I was writing this scene, because I had never experienced anything this pure in my life, but here, even the writer stepped aside, not wanting to mess with perceptions. Satisfied to experience, and nothing more.

When she laid back and spread herself, I eased my erection into her. There was a moment where we both gasped, smiled, kissed, and gasped some more with each liquid smooth thrust. Everything about the way she felt, the heat of her, the firmness and even the look in her eyes when they opened after an increasingly more urgent thrust, annihilated me in ways I welcomed. I saw in her chipped jade eyes, the tease of fulfillment, opening to see me staring at her, my gaze meeting hers, wishing I could stay forever in her hypnotic embrace.

As our pace quickened, I felt the darkness join in…

"It's not the darkness, Derek," she said, as if she had again read my mind. Perhaps we had moved beyond physical connection and into the realm of telepathy. I would have smiled if not for the edge to her statement; as if something more was to be revealed.

The silence came alive, as if awakened. I sensed an awakening. A hum blossomed, still a remnant of silence, yet less heard, more tactile. Sound as a tangible physical presence. The sound had a barely perceptible vibratory quality.

It reminded me of breathing.

She pulled me to her, my weight crushing her, enfolding her, her breasts yielding pillows, not so soft; a natural firmness accentuated their spherical shape. The nipples scrunched to a point that threatened to draw blood. Our urgent pace slowed again. It ached even more as we did this. I moaned, my whole body wanting to explode, not simply out of orgasmic inevitability, but more so for the sheer mountain-scaling magnitude of sensations that rippled through it. Alethea moaned as well, her neck stretched taut as her head tilted back.

In this life, this was as close to being at one with another as I had ever thought imaginable.

Somehow, she spoke, a tickle to my ear. "Remember I said I had sensed something resonating from Frank's place, something wrong?" I nodded, staring into her eyes, sensing the pure unfiltered passion and pleasure reflected within them, as well as something that nipped at the edges; something—

"I should have known it wasn't Frank's place where the sensation centered, it was *out here*."

I reared up again, slightly, to look into her eyes and decipher the codes there, something deeper, but then her head tilted back again, her neck so taut I thought it might disengage, sprout legs and run off, much as had happened in John Carpenter's *The Thing*. I furiously flushed this image from my head, wondering how such a monstrous recollection could intrude on my thoughts at a time like this.

Yet something *was* askew.

Shaking the disruption, I said, "The forest?"

Our voices were whispers, a contrast to the sporadic vocalizations of bliss as it scaled our spines and bloomed in our heads, our loins—the whole of us.

The forest responded, the ground fluid as a wave on waking seas, the vibration beneath forcing a swell to rise, but only slightly.

The hum *breathed* more rapidly.

We were too locked in to stop anything in motion. I knew no matter what she didn't want me to stop, by the pressure of her fingers on my back, sliding to my buttocks, and the strength of those fingers, plying me, pulling me into her, wanting me embedded within.

As one, I thought. As one.

"Not as one, this is your battle," she said, as ecstasy clawed at her words, the contrast confusing me. Despite the dogged impulsion that spurred us on, I had to internally question: should I stop or *must* I go on?

The ground continued to undulate, swaying to our rhythm, joining us, a ménage a trois enveloping myself, Alethea, and nature. The hum grew stentorian, no longer satisfied with simply breathing. The forest had chosen this strange noise as its voice. A noise like nothing I had ever heard before, yet it seemed to relate to Alethea's vocals on the recordings she had made, giving voice to whatever essence was present out here.

Coyotes bayed in the distance. The sounds reverberated through us, as if dictating the path our passion should or, more precisely, *would* take.

It was magnificent, the way the world seemed in tune with what we were exploring in each other.

And it was frightening, the way this part of the world seemed in tune with what we were exploring in each other.

I sensed the trees around us moving, sensed the life force within them. I acknowledged a wayward motivation as they leaned over us as if watching, prompting.

"This place," she said, breath hitching, voice straining, her orgasm escalating, ready for release. "This place, the phenomenology... vibrations... not audio, like my interests... pursuits"—panting; eager, yet anxious—"not magic... maybe magic, like that, it's... the trees, the inherent architecture of the landscape itself, maybe... mythology, maybe... something else— *something more—* "

I had no idea how she could talk or even attempt to make sense of it all. It seemed as if she forced herself to, as if it was necessary, cutting into the sensations that crackled as ecstasy uncoiled within her, awaiting release. My thoughts were spinning as well. Though side-tracked and stumbling with drunken abandon to comprehend Alethea's new input, they were still throwing off sparks that hinted at release. Even if I wanted to talk, the function was disabled, on hiatus.

The forest shook, no simple rolling waves, it shook with vengeance, something of our coupling, or perhaps Alethea's words, inspiring anger in it. I sensed and knew it was anger. My orgasm locked into motion, a strange way to think of it, but it had a starting point, and it was there, and now—

Alethea's eyes grew wide, the vines on her shoulders twitched as many spiders' legs. The forest kicked again, a baby about to be born. Or maybe out of pleasure. But pleasure for nature, what would that be? The coyote's sculpted savage symphonies with every howl. The fierce, soul-baring horn of my throat joined in the disharmonic orchestra as my orgasm achieved momentum amidst the mounting madness, almost...almost...

"Don't let it take you," Alethea said, the vines sinking into her flesh, pulling her *into* the ground, the haphazardly placed clothing and her flesh dissolving, her pleasure exploding through us even as this happened. I'd never even imagined anything of such force, such life affirming and life-releasing force. Go ahead, take me now, God, if you really are out there, take me, there can be nothing more to experience. But no, she'd said not to let it take me. It—*Nature*? Of course, but what could it do? These questions, surging and chaotic and enigmatic all at once, died as I thought of the possibilities, of magic, of the way Alethea was not just flowing but swimming through me, her spirit, even as she had disintegrated below me, the vines still squirming, the soil churning as if alive. The vines of her waist pulled at my buttocks, my legs, dragging me into that living earth. But she was gone, one with that earth, with nature. And I was naked, still feeling her wrapped around me, my orgasm affecting every molecule of me, everything on fire, in conflict. A dry ice explosion: every nerve suckled by the mouths of angels; demons; the unknown. The thought of breathing smoke as real as the thought that my screams could birth supernovas. Alethea gone yet

I still felt her, felt the unseen flesh amidst sensory overload, over n—

—outside the realm of possibility—

Crack.

The pain only ratcheted up the pleasure, the visceral upheaval, as if my bones were in revolt, rebelling against their uniform structure, punching out of the fleshprison, no parole passed, this was a daring escape signifying the audacity of something so unpredictable taking place. And me, the witness and playground to this unpredictable exhibition, first with Alethea's physical diffusion—and her seeming knowledge that something was about to happen that could not be stopped—and now, with my *transformation* (why this thought, this possibility?—because all bets were off), or simply death.

A sound emanated from within me, the orgasmic overtones strangled by the primal as it surged through me, sounding vaguely as Alethea had in her music, but so different in texture as to render my vocalization a singular statement on the transformation in progress. The sound was whittled from pain and pleasure as they danced within my mind, my body, my soul. It was the ultimate of either sensation I had ever experienced, conceived and, again, jutting from my back—

Crack.

Erupting as a volcano, but no lava in the making, no flow. This was blunt force. This was insistent without hesitation. I reached back to touch the impossible—a branch ripping through the flesh, sinew and muscle wrapped around the base—

Crack.

Another branch, erupting from the tattoo, the old tree tattoo. Branches were tearing through my flesh, this tree of life transformed into a killing force, it seemed: a tree of death. A literal birth of the tree sped up to mock the laws of nature, a time-lapse travesty. The laws of nature, shattered. I am the flashpoint intersection of what I had thought was reality, as intruded upon by the most absurd of fantasy, the tattoo a blueprint for what was in motion.

Always in motion, the world, nature, life—

Crack.

I screamed, the pain and pleasure beyond comprehension, the branches now shooting through everywhere, seemingly random but I am sure of a purpose. This is where they belong: this branch, and *this* one.

It was too much but it was not enough. I wanted it all, this feeling heightened by the darkness, the shadows hidden within the shadows, the sensation that the whole of life was flowing through me, my achingly erect penis buried in the soil, yet with each spasm, I take root in the soil, the soil welcoming me to a new beginning.

Blood and sweat, sticky on my flesh; flesh being overrun by more branches, each one an explosion of pain that demanded death, yet pleasure hooked in and demanded more—please, do it again: don't stop. Is this demand the most demonstrative call to self-flagellation imaginable? I think not, this was not some petty, faux ritual. This was something *more real* than the breath that filled my lungs, my lungs—

Crack.

I sensed insanity was the only step left, no one could ever feel this alive, and wanting death, and wanting more life, as if I was being reborn, but this not one based on religious fallacy, on promises of something more, afterwards. No, this was of another life, this one, earthbound, completely earthbound.

The complete thrust of my transformation digs in and takes hold. My senses shifted, became different, taking on a different resonance, a different vibration. My body was still with me—I know I am flesh, I know I am meat—but my new body was digging roots, the thighs and penis sprouting roots as I thrust into the soil. I am still orgasmic, but the matters of the flesh have been relegated to insignificance amidst the transformation. I still feel Alethea's vagina squeezed tight around me though I see nothing but dirt below me, yet the soil has a sensation that is beyond even her perfection, something alive within the moist dirt, the way it clumps, the way it takes me in, assists as *my* roots burrow deep into the earth.

The cracking is in full force—a Fourth of July firecracker celebration; a crowded gun range; a beatnik fingersnapping encore (what a joke, that one, but I am beyond omission: "Let my thoughts flow, they have never felt this free!")—the whole of my body transforming. I am beyond understanding, but understand this much: I am becoming one not with Alethea, but with nature.

I am taking shape, growing exponentially with every crack, sensing in ways never imagined, but too confusing to even absorb right now. All I have right now, this second, which is the only second that has ever mattered, until it is slaughtered by the one that follows it, and the next, is transformation, and even though my life has been driven by imagination, this was beyond even the feeble ministrations of my hot-wired brain. This was pure experience, without thought driving it or censoring it. This was stream-of-consciousness; this was true living.

I screamed again, the forest using my larynx as it had used Alethea's, a proclamation of primordial allegiance, of limbic comprehension. Coyotes accompanied my utterance with a chorus, something more felt than heard, their symphonic aptitude replaced by this more distinctly vocal transformation. Everything in transformation, it seemed. I did not actually hear it at all, yet I felt it resonate within the bark that encompassed my soul, or whatever remained...

Inside

"I continue working further away from being human and more toward *becoming* the primal scream."
—Jarboe

17: The Tree

—alive—

    —i am—that is all i know—colors abound—new and strange colors—so alien—never have i felt bathed in such luminescence—such kaleidoscopic wonder—prisms like mirrors—forever multiplying the scope of a single known color into every conceivable distortion—permutation—realization—colors whose pigments send messages that fuel internal mental engines—instinct—maybe—angles sharp and angles bending in ways never viewed with my eyes—my human eyes—and how am i seeing now—this explosion—this dizzying array of beams pouring out everywhere—over everything—beams burning brightly before reflecting off of mottled surfaces—changing—always changing—mirrors tilted to and fro—how am i able to see these colors—i sense—sensation—the one thing I am aware of—my senses—raging—but my senses are *different*—not distinctly *mine*—they are more indicative of the space i occupy—this space—the genius loci—amidst nature—it seems—i know this because *it is*—that is all—by rote—engrained in my soul—which is not exactly the proper word to define this as well—soul—i sense the human part of me is still present—yet it struggles with understanding this new self—the transformation that has transpired—the internal files of knowledge that i have collected over the forty years of my existence have been leeched of everything and i have absolutely no idea how to express this transformation—but my brain still works as it always has worked—so it plows on—forging through as best it can—so—vision—cluttered—confusing—shards of images—not images—colors—that sculpt angles—that send messages—my thoughts my own—but my thoughts also littered with the inception of that which infiltrates—in touch with the nature of all that is around me—and it comes to me—what i see is what they see—animals—birds—insects—this is what penetrates my thoughts with their own thoughts—more so—their impressions—they don't think—per se—but there is *something*—their nature—the nature of what they are—me—amidst nature—these animals—birds—insects—these colors that overwhelm are hypersensitive observational receptions—perceptions—conceptions—the herky jerky movements—sudden instances of crystal clarity—but clarity not as i know it—but as *they* know it—i drown in this one sensation—the colors—unseen wavelengths made visible for me—by their eyes—and their ideals—ha—no—that cannot be—they cannot think—truly think—and it comes to me then—more understanding—their thoughts are not thoughts—none of them—their brains too small or virtually none at all—or maybe it is the way i comprehend them—perhaps—but i sense the primeval—that which drives them—the colors bleed and shimmer as patterns—designs—their purpose woven into the reticulated system that unceasingly dances in their world—and i sense more—feel myself crawling through the muck of my brain—maybe i am the lesser being and they—all of them—animal—bird—insect—have something more cherished in a way—something so simple that it makes their life something of force—not filled with nonsense—with compromise—i feel as though i am drowning in the possibilities—immersed to the brim and no way to climb out—over the rim—there is no rim—there is only the climbing—even smell is altered to the point that it is more something seen and not sniffed—i cannot put this in a place where understanding is even within reach—but smell is around me and as with sight—it is something that is only ingested within the crux of need—nothing more—there is hunger—this much i know—this is not something of which uncertainty participates—there is hunger—but as with everything else—it is part of the process of their lives—their living—it is the driving force—concentrated—polished—perfect—something to be admired—envied—this focus—their urges—for lack of the right word—for i do not speak their language—i am sure they would have some other way of expressing this better than i can—but i would not understand that either—or—perhaps—they find the necessity for definition—for breaking it all down and defining it further—pointless—obsolete—they are that focused—their urges—are all they really have—and now—i know the part of me that thinks—that perceives—is corrupting the sensations—streamlining them to fit what i know—this is both necessary for that part of me that is human—and sad because i can sense something within being eroded—that something—the perfection of life as it is—and nothing more—but—within my brain—within this body i have—this new body—i sense a glimmer of control—of being able to move between an animal—bird—and insect—to center my reception—to focus—somehow—and the shards of color become singular—not the maddening—fragmentary funhouse that has battered me since i awoke—

—was i asleep—is this what i have always been—is this where i was always meant to be—the fragmentary becomes singular—sight—smell—instinct—everything—even that which evades description—but—i am sure—is a major part of the whole of me—and i follow one wave—my eyes—the eyes of my host—i sense it is a bird—but cannot turn its head to look at its body—control on that level is not mine to wield—yet—the ripples and angles and messages the wave sends to the host—and i see something flutter within the wave—corruption again—of this perfect color that is not color—and i sense the hunger and—

—gone...

...i do not understand and then understanding comes to me...a wave of understanding like the drowning waves of colors around me...

...that which i had focused with has left me...my body...driven by the hunger i sensed course through its being...so the momentary disorientation is flooded with the influx of everything else that touches me...

...and I smile...

...not a physical expression, for there is no countenance upon which the visual impression can be articulated...but the joy of finding another host, of focusing with it and the inception of revelatory things never imagined, fills me with such jubilation I want to burst with the incomprehensible input, but that is also not on the agenda…but—

Life is. Life around me and life so perfect I would cry, but tears are also no longer a part of the battery of responses that I have dominion over. They are not a part of me, of what I am and what I can physically do in this foreign, alien, never even considered state.

My imagination cannot stretch that far, but—

What can I actually do physically?

I sense myself stretching, but not really stretching. I feel myself flow through me, taking all of me in, yet the physicality of the act is impossible to register as actually *happening*. I am confined to that which I am *within*, but exist in ways that expand the chains of confinement to a place of infinite inclusion of *everything*.

I am the earth.

I am the sky…the air…

I am everything and everywhere. I would say godlike, but even that does not embrace the totality of consciousness that engulfs me.

My hunger feeds deep in the ground, the roots of me nurturing me, the warmth and vitality of soil wrapped so tight around me…and I also sense heat from above.

I sense the tips of the tallest branches reaching, growing the tiniest iota every nanosecond, though the noticeable changes may take years, yearning for the sun that batters them with rays of absolute radiance (color, yes, but so much more than color: nourishment, vitality). I succumb to the sheer audacity of heat distilled as light (as taste as smell as…), of the thrilling sear of color as it caresses me and sinks in, as if alive itself. It is a warmth that defines life. It is a warmth that cowers meagerly at the foot of anything I ever have imagined. The most far-fetched fantasy cannot compare—

Have I ever really imagined? Has my life as a writer—no—*as a human being,* been nothing more than prelude to the true definition of life—*of being alive*—that I am experiencing right now?

It is all too much.

It is all so perfect.

It overwhelms, it enthralls.

I am in awe!

I am alive.

I am!

Then—

—a touch perceived as cold, dead, yet with the contact, the thought *extinguished*, and something I can fully understand. All elation withers as cold human flesh presses against my hide.

Through mysterious machinations I expect never to understand, I have been inexplicably transformed into a tree, perhaps an old tree much as the tattoo on my back: the tattoo a blueprint for the attainment of the impossible. But I am something more, something of actual substance and not just imagination, three-dimensional, tangible if I could feel me. Something else does, and the touch siphons all of that which is good in my new state and like a vacuum it sucks me into a place that is fraught with thoughts that I can understand, yet do not want to.

Images, not from the eyes, but the mind: of blood, madness, perversion. Images that even in their depravity I can understand. Images that remind me of when I was human.

I see Alethea, but it is a different interpretation, younger but unmistakably her, as if this being knew her then—before—but has not seen her for many years. And even at that, the recollection is distorted, scarred by a brain that sees things in terms drenched in ugliness, in blotchy charcoal hues rubbed clean of happiness or even hope. This being, the owner of this diseased brain, sees things shaded with black rust that infects perception, its interpretation of her so very different, as if she is something abhorrent, something horrible. Then I realize it is not something abhorrent, it is not something horrible, it is the magnitude of loneliness and wanting that has tarnished this recollection of Alethea. This being has made her something detestable because that is the only way it can move forward, yet the damaged status of its brain has rendered healing, hence, moving forward, an impossible endeavor.

Infinitely flipping a coin, looking for the proper advantage— best two out of three; best five out of nine; best one billion out of...—yet unable to find an advantage that works properly within its damaged psyche.

I understand this because this being is human, and even as polluted as its brain is, it is still human. As I once was and wish never to be again.

That is when I sense that this being is, obviously, Aleister Blut, the escaped madman, though this recognition does not register as I glean the thoughts. Another name sporadically rises to the forefront, as if Aleister Blut was never there: Alexander Burroughs. Yet with *this* identification, *this* name—this other side to the coin of personality that flips with feverish determination; flipping without revealing heads or tails; flipping because that is what it does, no proper advantages taken here, either—is mercilessly elbowed to the rear, beaten down and battered, vanquished and forgotten.

But it does land, this coin. It sits on its ridge, allegiance undecided.

The black rust corrodes everything.

I wonder how he could so absolutely cleanse Aleister Blut from his thoughts, his life, if that part of his personality was such a pertinent part, for so long.

And how could the person he has been his whole life be demoted to a place of such irrelevance?

I seek passage through the tendrils that connect the brain to the eyes, moving through him, and see in ways that are different, yet much more to my understanding than with the birds that have been my most focused visual interpreters so far. I see colors that are more familiar to me, and trees, birds, dirt and…

His mind intrudes again: it is a roller-coaster, something to behold, a different kind of standardized disorientation. This is the way it always is, within the decrepit mental minefield, every thought punctured, a Swiss cheese array of black holes littered along the gray matter wasteland. This mind is warped, the thoughts sprinkled with grimy dreams, caustic glimpses that have no foundation in reality as I know it, though under the circumstances, what do I honestly know? I sense the desire to be completely free of self, as if the self is gangrenous and it wants to cut it out. I sense a need for nothing, the unquenchable gist of nothing, of blending in and never acknowledging either of the personas that have resided in its flesh. A white light flashbulb "pop" glimmer of

Aleister Blut, a live snapshot amidst on-stage tedium and a sudden shock of amplified noise that I actually hear (I can hear his thoughts, the scenes as they play out in his head), rides shotgun with another photo, this one older: a child with a crooked smile and bright eyes. One can easily surmise that this child will dance with anarchy, with purposeful anarchy, but that purpose will stagger as dissatisfaction and cloying media expectations destroy the dreams that hum merrily along for an instant as I take in that gleefully selfless face.

The crooked smile in the photo reveals the burgeoning dreams of youth, and a history as yet lived, but knowledge after the fact meshes everything into a stew of confusion.

The coin totters, tips to one side, lands flatly with dull, apathetic intent.

As Aleister Blut peers into another mental pothole, I see Alethea again, and do not want to see her this way. I somehow, through strength of will, gather the wherewithal to pull out of his masochistic excursion into self-torture and, with the avoidance, I sense consternation, I sense a *vibration*, and that part of what remains of Aleister Blut screams.

Sight again, and sound, the voice, the scream. I feel it as much as I hear it, the audio rampage released. Aleister Blut's unrestrained fury pulls us out of his personal abyss. Alexander is gone, Aleister reigns, completely. He twirls and I see trees, sunbeams slicing through, and crepuscular flashes like long, lamp-lit tubes. Dust and debris and pollen—the seeds of life—float through the staggered rays of light.

Aleister reaches out to wave a hand through the light, creating a condensed tornado with the brief movement.

He laughs, this moment something to cherish.

This moment—gone.

He twirls again, one or the other hand on my wooden hide, staying connected, as if he understands that there is something more happening here, and staying attached to *this* tree invites the other one—me—into his mind and body.

He looks up and I see the majesty of me, a huge tree, gnarled, twisted at the mossy base, many huge branches reaching out long and strong, while tinier branches can be spotted further up me, as the height of me is visually scaled.

I am beautiful. I am robust and mighty. I am ancient and newborn.

I am.

He glances down and around me, at that mossy base, and I (technically we) see ivy wrapped around the base of me. *Ivy that moves.* He awkwardly shuffles his feet away from it, fearful of its touch. I do not fear the embrace. It is rather comforting, if comfort is a possibility in this new existence.

Suddenly he turns again, scanning the forest, the empty patch, and I sense it in his belly: anticipation.

Whispering: "Alethea." I hear it from the outside, with his ears: his voice, a rasp, a weed scratching at pavement, struggling for sunlight. I hear it inside, the ego-altered perception, one of strength, one of intent.

Anticipation peaks, but no mental pictures accompany the sensation, to give it shape, to alleviate the trepidation. But it is resolute, whatever inspires this anticipation, and it is inevitable.

The earth rumbles, as it did last night, or was that many years ago? My core clenches, that part of me which remembers being human, remembers fear. It is the concrete acknowledgement that some *thing* is on the way. Some *thing* is about to be born.

18: Disconnect

Tension taut as a noose, yet I'm able to slip my neck out of the loop by aligning my thoughts with those of Alethea. She might believe anything was possible, but she was not blind to the possibility that it was not. Within her beliefs, she incorporated and interpreted as was necessary for the person she is because she loves life, much as I do.

Here, now, I am being shown things that both corroborate her belief systems and validate something more horrid: the existence of something that has no conscience, no empathy. Nature, but not of a condition I would consider as normal, though, of course, how am I to actually know the ideologies exacted within nature? I cannot (until now, I think; *until now*). What I sense is something more avaricious, something of an infected magnetism that Aleister senses as well, though less clearly. His thoughts boil over with despair, disorder, and dread.

Aleister pulls away from me and in that instant, I am nothing but what I am. A tree, this huge, beautiful tree that seems to have been here for ages, but has in reality been here for, as far as I can tell, only a handful of hours, though time is also something that moves differently here, my perceptions perhaps shaped by the difference.

I am completely aware that things move different in nature, time has a life of its own, it is not a construct of human invention, it is eternal and ephemeral at once. It contains eons long dead and futures yet birthed.

I know that this tree has always been me and I have always been this tree. Now that I am here, I have always been a part of this place.

I know the secrets that roam freely here, and the secrets that struggle to stay hidden forever, for their deeds are of a more conspiratorial design.

I know that this place in which I reside—the peaceful me; the flabbergasted and joyous me—is alive and its dreams are malignant and insatiable. (I also know that it is not the only place in this world like this: alive. I am reminded of Auschwitz.) It wants something that only the minds of those who venture within range can give it.

It is shaping these thoughts into realization, giving them substance, plausibility.

Aleister touches me again, a violent shudder of understanding that what is in motion is a product of Frank's warped mind, my slightly off center observations, Aleister's (and Alexander's, I'm sure) madness, and Alethea, somehow. Maybe the beauty of me now? Maybe something else.

The vibrations around me hum with life, though not like before. I hadn't felt them as I do now, yet know they have been here all along. What was it that Alethea had hinted at before the world went sideways and down the rabbit hole? The phenomenology of nature, of the forest here, as if the organic architecture of the trees and landscape has somehow awakened something within this place and it has grown hungry and needs minds to feed on. Minds that it takes from and shapes from and realizes as mass, as real. Not just figments of imagination, it re-constitutes itself with the thoughts but, being nature (without conscience, without rules—there are no "laws of nature"—nature *is*, nothing more), it finds the base thoughts the most intrinsic and realistic, because they have been with us and with the earth the longest. Not exactly evil or negative, but driven by instinct as *modus operandi* to being, and, yes, maybe evil and negativity are the foundation because they lack logic, lack anything of consequence. They are the building blocks that instigated the creation of man, electrical impulses sparking within primordial sludge, prompting evolution, as fueled by the primary nuclei tandem, to procreate and to feed. The necessity to feed accentuated by the singular requirement: to kill.

Only recently has this requirement been put in a place where controlled circumstances allowed continuation amidst the unspoken edicts of social order via slaughterhouses and such. Evolution or intelligence or dumb luck, we became civilized. Though, of course, the *act* of killing still interferes with the social order as we humans slip all the time, killing each other out of anger, lust, madness, or pleasure.

Nature, on the other hand...nature *is*, nothing more. Its aspirations are simple. It is a child forever.

I realize that my perceptions may be skewed as well, thinking of nature as malignant and insatiable.

It just wants to live.

It welcomes whatever is next, be it tranquility or murder. *This place* prods the latter, the food chain dynamics prompted by survival, accentuated by bloodlust. I wonder if the influence extends to the animals, birds, and insects at an accelerated rate here.

Through Aleister's eyes, I see it, twenty feet or so from us, bubbling up from the ground, something the bright neon yellow color of bile.

Leaning toward a question: "Alethea" —

—our connection broken. I hear, as the animals and birds hear, something more like a shove than a sound; many connections lost. I sense the birds have left me. Then—

—re-connected again, and Aleister is looking up at me and my beauty is blurred as his eyes are moist, touched by anger or fear or simply tears, I am not sure. His thoughts are swarming as many black flies at a landfill buffet, too many to distinguish one from the other.

He yells: "Why have you stopped?"

I do not know what he means.

He turns and that which was bubbling has stopped, but only for a moment. The moment of our disconnection, perhaps.

It re-commences with bubbling, the humming amplifies with weight, as if the sound—which I hear now, in his ears; it is not just a vibration, it is a sound—grows in volume and substantiality as the ground rumbles. The evolution of the hum, maybe? I am reminded, for reasons I cannot explain, of birth. (A thought I'd had before my transformation, of something being born.) The ground is giving birth, but to what?

It bubbles up, this vile blinding color, thick and viscous. It pulses through the ground, dirt crumbling around it, eager to give it the space it needs to take shape.

The ground is leaking, a wound in need of stanching and tightly sewn stitches.

Amorphous, throbbing sickly, we watch the liquid swell, spreading, *growing*, still lurching out of the ground. It does not flow, this liquid. There is *physicality* to its movement. A few sections jiggle like bloated blubber, a sense of perversion beyond conception.

I feel, within Aleister, fear and wonder. And more black holes gasping for life within his brain.

Something rips through the seething muck, but does not leave it, still a part of it. And another. Shapes that, upon tearing through the glutinous liquid, pull mucus-like strands from their bodies. A dim suggestion of shapes that have a familiarity I know jut from this massive pool of mental sickness made real.

A flashing thought of my own design: suppose this place, as I understand it, manifests something from the minds of those who traverse here. Isn't that what Frank said? Suppose blending two minds really messes up the chemistry? And, in reality, more than two minds.

I sense the adrenaline surging through Aleister as if it is my own. He is excited, bewildered, worried, afraid, and completely insane, as evidenced by some of the thoughts I can latch on to in his head, not even distinct any more. The thoughts as black flies have mutated into fat bees, congealing as a hive-mind collective, and something comes clear in my scope of understanding, of another murder on his way here, as if he is distracted by this, the clothing he wears. I see the too baggy slacks and the plaid shirt as images in his head, but not with his eyes as they are focused on the heaving yellow pool.

Old memories mingle with new memories, dreams and desires squeeze between the margins. It is impossible to make sense of the deluge, but the primal gist of Aleister's being shines through, even amidst the chaos. I sense a fuzzy perceptual glitch that flits through the thoughts, lending them possibilities that memories lack, of undefined quests he wants to undertake. I sense both the need to help and the need to destroy, the conflict writhing as a paper bag full of maggots on a hot summer's day.

Again, the younger version of Alethea comes into focus, and he is having sex with her, a markedly different approach than what she and I had consummated last night, this one rough, fueled by desperation and nothing more. I know his body as if it is my own, see it naked and see Alethea as well. I watch him, her puppet, Alethea pulling the strings. This thought disturbs me, but I know it is a perceptual anomaly, the perceptions of a person who is remembering and embellishing at the same time, the memories of before as captured, tortured, and destroyed by the overwhelming mental corruption in which black holes breathe with sour breath that, even in his mind, I can almost make out the smell.

If they ever had anything between them it is not what I see here, in his head. This is what loneliness and insanity do to memories, making them more nightmare than truth.

At least, that is what frolicking through his madness inspires me to think, or hope.

Then, there is a moment that I understand as love, unscathed by the insanity that surrounds it, allowed to stand tall because it is the only thing that links Aleister to what it means to be human, or at least the illusion of being human. It is precious, this moment, and under the circumstances, stunning.

There is so much contradiction it rises like floodwaters, threatening to drown me.

He releases his touch and I am thrown, this time vertigo has embraced me and is taking me for the ultimate ride, this one to the heart of the earth, a place where all dreams and fantasies and madness await birth —

—he touches me, and I immediately understand. That thing taking form before us is only allowed to take form when we are connected.

We watch as one of the things jutting out from the blob speaks: "Madness lubricates the soul. My brain greased with desires, physical degradation found between the legs of my prey or riding the spine of the needle. You never really got me, Derek. You got lost in my eyes and between my thighs, but refused to go all the way down. Until now."

Our eyes take in this shape. Our ears take in the words, the nasal whine clipped with a degree of spite. It does not look like her, but that voice, those words: ex-wife number two, Asia, has somehow been born of this madness and is taking form before our astonished eyes. This is my perception. Aleister is completely lost.

The shape strips off more of the clotted layers, and it is not Asia I see, but ex-wife number one, Doreen.

Asia's voice again, from Doreen's mouth: "Scraping bottom or fucking my ass, now you get both but cannot fulfill your prophecy, Derek. Unless we can get Aleister Blut there to handle the heavy work."

The thing that looks vaguely like Doreen, still buried waist deep in the boiling liquid—human oil? Skin cream afterbirth?— massages its breasts with lewd precision.

Aleister recoils at the speaking of his name, a split second retreat into his buried other half, Alexander. A split second of absolute nothingness, but I also sense his loins awakening. He yells out, "Where is Alethea?" but as distraction, his brain implodes, overtaken by tattered rhythms and wily lyrics that have nothing to do with Dark Angel Asylum's crisp observations of a world gone mad. These lyrics are of a more personal apocalypse, his lost soul in search of something, love or salvation perhaps, or just searching through the wires of synaptic damage for something to hold on to, a tightrope dance born of disorder. How could this thing being vomited from the ground know me, he thinks, a sliver of clarity, and back to the noisy rhythmic onslaught in his head, and now lyrics, more screamed than sung in his voice: "*No more rules and regulations/slaughtered here your destination/chiseled on the walls of time/no future here, not yours or mine.*"

What Asia speaks with Doreen's tongue, as crossed with Aleister's crazed but eerily succinct lyrics, makes my thoughts reel and my brain ache.

My brain in this tree. I still sense my body. I know how a body works. *I am.* Does the mode of transference go both ways? Can I manipulate Aleister as one would a puppet, as he falsely remembered Alethea had done with him?

One of the other lumps rising from the muck tears off sticky clumps and speaks: "The least you could have done was give me the right body." Doreen's strong voice expresses exasperation, while the body writhes unappealingly, taking shape as Asia, and possibly many others.

I wonder if this place is enjoying the absurdity on parade.

The two naked forms, as seen with Aleister's eyes, continue to try to pull themselves from the muck, but both remain stuck at the waist, unable to make any headway.

"My dirty hole awaits your friend, Derek. Or, should I say, Doreen's dirty fucking hole. Maybe he can inject me with the appropriate filth to justify this preposterous allocation of form. We'll rehab in Hell, you and me; we'll dine on shit and love it, loverboy. We three or four or the more the merrier. Who's next to join the fray, Derek?"

Three more figures rise up, but Aleister's brain pushes the images away, turning away. I appreciate the break, but know it cannot last. More noise, more distraction from his head: "*All the dreams and all the hope/shattered like a scarred glass globe/no more time, no dawn tomorrow/Alethea's fate is wrapped in sorrow.*"

The mention of Alethea steers my thoughts toward her, but squealing feedback and pummeling percussion override my focus.

"Alethea's close by. You need to shut this down. Before it gets really sticky." Doreen's voice sending me a warning.

Aleister swings his head toward the Asia thing from which Doreen's voice had spoken; the almost-Asia thing.

It registers in his head to ask, "Where is Alethea?" but, astonishingly, I am able to transfer my question to his lips: "Really sticky? Is Alethea in danger?"

I didn't ask, "How do you know of Alethea?" Under the circumstances, why wouldn't she know Alethea? Nonetheless, the mention of things getting really sticky required my attention, especially with Alethea's present absence.

(She disintegrated into the ground, right? *Maybe...* What am I to really believe at this point anyway?)

Feedback rises with exponential ferocity, all instruments as channeled through amplifiers turned to Spinal Tap's comically infernal eleven, in the red, and drawing blood just to match the madness of his derailing thoughts.

Asia's retort, spat from Doreen's mouth, passing by lips which never would have spoken of such disgusting things. "Sticky is a goal in life, eh, Derek? Aleister? Impale me with your erection, fill me with your manjuice drug of life, heroin babies await the—"

"Get a hold of yourself before..." Doreen says, the words dying in Asia's mouth as her face contorts.

"Yes, get a hold of yourself because we're about to open the gates to Frank's macabre mental playground," Asia says, her spiteful nasal whine underscored by the sudden insertion of Frank's forever ex, Carissa, into the mix. Carissa's drama queen theatrics as channeled through Doreen's mutating body via flamboyant arm waving, always one for broad gesticulations, as if she were a model presenting something: here, behind door number 1...

She stops, becomes a statue; a gargoyle in sullen observance. And something punches through one of the shapes, instantly ripping the sheet of slime, as if this shape has a purpose that the other shapes can only imagine fulfilling.

I had almost forgotten about Frank, but with the addition of Carissa's twitchy insect theatrics, and the addition of this new yet somewhat familiar shape, I am reminded that this place, this forest of the bizarre, is hooked deep into his tainted mind as well as whatever I am experiencing or influencing. Whatever all of my disparate collaborators are influencing.

The shape that pulls itself out of the muck is quick to stand on its own legs. It steps from the boiling mass and as it does, the other shapes, Doreen and Asia and the two other blobs without distinguishing features, slump lifeless upon its exit.

The shape stretches, the mucus-like coating congealing as pools at its feet. It doesn't even need to pull it off as the others had attempted, it patiently waits for it to drip to the ground. It would be hard for it to do, anyway, as only one hand would be able to help in the cleansing.

The other hand extends out as an axe, the arm morphing at the wrist, the wrist elongating, and at the end there is a huge axe head. It is something of force, strength, threat. Something of purpose.

"Izzy?" I ask, using Aleister's mouth again. Aleister recedes into himself, joining Alexander in hiding, lost to events as they dance the dance of the strange all about him.

"Who were you expecting, Average Joe?"

The laughter that follows has nothing to do with Izzy's playful, perpetually sixteen-year-old goofball laughter. It is the laughter of Average Joe, if Average Joe were made human.

The other figures had been part of my real world. Average Joe was purely fictional, but I banked on him being as much a part of Frank's world as any real person. This would explain his presence here, if explanations were even a viable consideration at this point.

The universal thought that binds Aleister and Alexander and me, at that moment, is *Shit!* As in oh-fucking-no this cannot be happening.

But it is. Standing naked before us, Average Joe wears Izzy's body, which makes sideways sense. After all, Frank had used Izzy in the construction of Average Joe. Except for the arm, *that arm*, the one being raised, flexing, growing accustomed to the weight, swinging it now—swish, swish—smiling, something so malicious Izzy could never have pulled it off.

And he is walking toward me, toward us, his determined strides pounding the dirt, the ground reverberant at his feet, through my roots.

Aleister scrunches down low, his physical body meeting with his already scrunched selves inside, hiding in plain sight, leaning against me, and at this moment, I wish he would disconnect.

I wish it all would disconnect.

19: The Axe

"Did I ever tell you the one about the horror writer and his most famous creation, a heartless flesh-bound killing machine?" There was a snippet of Izzy in the asking, but the eyes, the look on his face: it was all Average Joe. And this was in no way remotely funny.

Through Aleister's eyes I watch as Average Joe swings the axe-arm all the way back to the ground, as if he is preparing to put all his might into the punch line, as well as my bark and moss covered hide.

Despite circumstances, I feel it quiver within me, this sense of my own body, which I had almost forgotten or abandoned amidst the joy of being transformed into a tree. I sense this act will slice into flesh and I will feel the brutal slash of pain with all my being. I sense within this fantastic madness the human me again, the human that I *still* am, more so than at any point in recent memory, even if that memory is only of the last few minutes, hours.

Aleister crumples even further down, physically and mentally, his hands now hovering over his face, feeble protection, as if this violence is directed at him. Voyeuristically, he watches the arm propel into action; *we* watch the arm propel into action.

Chips of bark fly, the axe-arm digs into my wooden husk. I sense it as if it hits my body in the chest, a visceral thump that ignites every nerve in a relay race away from the source of impact, the breastbone—

I scream, the sound shoved out from within Aleister's throat. The inflection of the tone, the timbres, and the cacophonous release, totally and completely foreign to anything Aleister has ever attempted. The feedback, which had sunk into a low gurgling equivalent of electricity awaiting inspiration, cranks to a shrill, deafening pitch that throbs, as if his brain is trying to puncture its way out of his skull, this whole thing too much, *too much*, for him to grasp. It is as if an orchestra of unknown instruments — this one indicative of fear, this one indicative of dread — has decided self-destruction to be the most logical translation of everything that it is experiencing right now.

The sound is an umbrella folding over us.

Average Joe pulls the axe-arm from my hide with much effort.

His smile is something of unmitigated delight.

He is erect with anticipation as he swings again —

Deeper still, this pain to the core, my heart stutters in panic, the metal of the blade caressing ruptured arteries, more bone, and much blood.

And, through Aleister's wavering, mutinous eyes, I see blood spouting out of my tree self.

All bets are *completely* off. I have no way to comprehend blood, like a gusher of sap, spouting from the wooden husk of me.

The noise wobbles, as if Aleister has no way to comprehend the sight before us as well. His brain goes completely black, shutting down. His eyes remain open, maybe because of our connection, but Aleister and Alexander have left the building, the forest, his skull, this scene.

It is all for me to watch…and feel.

A need to scream is quashed as the ripped circuitry in Aleister's head somehow disallows me anything more than his eyes. I do scream, but it is something buried within me, yet release is silently attained, pushing out of the most prominent opening within my wooden body, the tear in my chest, my hide. My scream expressed as spurting arches of blood, painting Average Joe in the adornments of my agony.

Average Joe laughs sadistically.

He swings swifter now, again and again, as if his goal is at hand and there is nothing but attainment and release left, a concentrated urgency much like the culmination of sex, and he stops, reaches into the ruptured hole and pulls with force (I feel it, this weight being shifted, torn), pulls with purpose (the weight pulsing, pumping), blood gushing in rivers, waterfalls along my bark, spilling onto Aleister.

I realize the only way to stop the madness is to do as Aleister (and the forgotten Alexander) has done, and shut myself down, my brain, let it go, fly with the birds, ride the wind, leave the premises...

As Average Joe pulls *my heart* from the belly of the tree, from the center of my chest, I force our eyes to look away, first to the ground, the base of me, and that strange, moving ivy. Then to the deepest heights of the sky, to the noon sun as it burns at the heart of this place, burns into our eyes, our mind, my mind, fly with the birds, ride the wind, rocket ship to the sun and sweet incineration, let it all burn...

It burns so bright.

I stare as it all goes a brilliant orange, red, yellow, so yellow, seeing the sun with human eyes, not the eyes of all around me, but human eyes. I stare, unwavering, as the blackness grows vast and eclipses it all.

20: Blue Metropolis

After an indeterminate spell, I am aware of warmth. I am aware of a blackness which does not burn, which only soothes. I am aware of light again, a sudden light—maybe this is consciousness awakening—and it burns, but the burn is gentler, an invitation: look what we have for you now, Derek.

My eyelids—*my eyelids*—pinched shut but sneaking a peek and in that instant something more assails me. I am trapped at the foot of an avalanche of smells (baked dough, human sweat, acrid piss, hot rubber on concrete) and sounds (the throaty bark of a dog, the abrasive squeal of automobile brakes, the murmur of voices locked in live conversations or just those on the other end of the blue tooth, the fluttering whoosh of distant helicopter blades) and touch (hard slab of warm concrete: my bed) and so much more as my eyes open to take in a city, not *the* City, not San Francisco, but one that is similar, another metropolis, perhaps Chicago, even New York.

Eye-level concrete, I am low to the ground. I see a dented green dumpster overflowing with rubbish: a stained and ripped mattress; open black plastic bags of garbage (more smells: dead spices, sour milk, stale alcohol, rot); splintered wood (a chair? a table?); torn cardboard; an endless outpouring of rubbish.

There is more, everywhere.

Colorful graffiti scribbled with care across the burnt sienna bricks of a Brownstone tenement to my left: indecipherable codes, the language of the street, three-dimensional block lettering that screams for attention; attention garnered, but to what avail? Sunlight dancing off the rusted steel skeletal frames of many fire escapes. Steam wriggling from the lip of a manhole, just like in every noir film ever made, but with the blanched tint of sunlight, the impression is less dynamic. Is this the *real* world? Automobiles whisking by beyond the entrance to the alley signal affirmation. Yes, this is an alley, not the forest. Multi-colored metallic beasts, some polished to pristine glare, others bruised, hulking forward with clanking effort, wishing to be put out to pasture indicate as much.

More sounds assail me. Horns bleating in anger or frustration, urgency or hello. The metronome bell-like bleat that signals to all a delivery truck is backing up, somewhere beyond my visual confirmation. A siren that speaks the syntax of warning and, again, urgency. It seems everybody is in a hurry to be somewhere else. People sloshing by, a river of flesh adorned in suits and ties, skirts and heels, leather and chains, stone-washed jeans and Doc Martens.

More smells congeal, feverishly aromatic. Cigarette smoke, some harsh, some clove sweetened. Deodorants, colognes and perfumes—citrus to berry to meadows or musky as an animal—masking sweat, but sweat is winning most battles.

I spot a body across the alley from me, indecipherable like the graffiti, but still adorned in the unspoken language of the city, of city life, the lost and lonely, a person covered in too much clothing, a scraggly beard like a twig and mud-pasted nest the only signifier of gender, sleeping or dead, slumped and silent. No sounds, not even breathing to be gleaned, but from this distance, the city sounds override everything.

There is the sudden realization that I am naked, my skin rubbed raw by scooting to a sitting position on the concrete before I stand and stretch. The sun feels wonderful, but the chill that accompanies it raises goose bumps all over my flesh and the realization that the impact of the chill is more profound because there is nothing shielding my flesh. Well, there is something. There is blood spattered across my chest.

At that moment, it all hits me, a rush like heroin the second the juice hits the vein. I remember brief bouts of heroin, and Asia. Asia who was talking through Doreen's body a few minutes ago or a *lifetime* ago, Christ. I take it all in, allowing this world to bulldoze into my reality.

How did I get here? Where is here? Where is Alethea? Where is everything else?

I was with Alethea in the forest, and then I was transformed, and then...

I duck behind the dumpster, suddenly aware that something is beyond amiss, it has taken the crazy train and dumped me here without my luggage, clothing, or the wherewithal to understand. As if anything since before the transformation and, really, anything since I have been visiting Frank, has made any sense.

An accented voice from above, not God or even one of His cohorts in the observatory of Heaven: "Hey, Louis, there's a fuckin' naked guy all bloody and shit out here."

Glancing in the direction of the voice, I see a windowsill decorated with potted plants, wilted and forgotten flowers, and a shadow moving behind a rippling white-sheet curtain.

I touch my chest, the blood dry, the surface firm. No evidence of an excavated heart.

Homeless guy across from me rearranges himself, more comfortable accommodations gathered as a sealed black plastic garbage bag that never made it to, or was fruitlessly escaping from, the dumpster, is nominated as a head rest, not really a pillow as something sharp pokes through one end. He sees me and closes his eyes, no notice registered, probably used to manifestations wild and hallucinatory anyway, this one rather boring, not a polka dotted elephant or a talking sofa.

"Fuckin' pervert. I'm callin' the cops." Another male voice, brusque, the unknown accent sharpened by his disgust.

I rifle through the garbage within reach, hoping for a pair of pants, but my quest is unfulfilled, as naked as my ass.

My brain is buzzing with the locomotive onslaught of this reality as crossed with the previous one...or two? The "real" reality of me and Frank and Alethea and Izzy. The bizarre yet felt-so-real reality of being a tree. Comprehension is somewhere to the left, out of reach. Decompression is mandatory. I have to come down to this place and take it for what it is, because something is in motion that makes no sense, yet I can feel and smell and see and hear and even taste (in my head; in my mouth) Alethea. My tongue is coated with sleep and the memories as sweet mist, as tooley fog creeping across the taste buds. If I remember that much, sense it so deeply, it must be asked, what is real anymore? Am I actually here, in this unknown city?

Am I actually here?

Am I even...

Two bodies approach, blue coated from head to toe, shields glimmering, holstered guns and batons: "What do we have here? Public nudity is a no-no."

The voice is familiar, though more lively than it has been in the few days I have stayed with him: Frank.

"Did I ever tell you the one about the guy who lost himself and didn't have any I.D. or a passport, birth certificate, or anything to indicate he was even himself?"

Izzy. Not Average Joe, but Izzy. The gleam in his eyes was mischievous, not malignant.

"Frank. Izzy. Guys, what's going on?"

Frank leaned into me and whispered: "You have the right to remain silent. Anything you say can and will be...you know the drill. You remember in King's *Desperation*, when the cop stops the couple and while he's doing the Miranda mambo, slips in, 'I'm going to kill you,' as if it's part of the deal? I won't say that. I have no intention of killing you. I have something more *ridiculous* in mind."

His smile threatened to split his face as a watermelon in summertime, quenching his madness. There was something sinister in his posture. The look in his eyes told the truth. Eyes like coals before the match has been struck. Dead, not real.

Not real.

They each took an arm and jerked me forward, me complaining all the way, naked and feeling more naked for the humiliation.

"Pardon us. Excuse us. We got ourselves a lost soul here. Let us through."

All the faces, whether the bodies were male or female, were the faces of those I had known in my life. Doreen and Asia, of course, and Jamaica Jennefer, Gina and Darlene, and others as well, my agent, my publicist, my kids (turn away, Claire, you don't want to see this), Carissa with a big smile of I-told-you-so spattered across her leering face, as if she'd ever told me anything. Celebrities and casual acquaintances and more, the one night stands, the friendships without intimacy, yet intimately close. They all seemed familiar, no matter their time in my head or heart, those who lingered and those with whom notice was barely taken.

But I did not see Alethea and that had to mean something.

I screamed, "No! when a child ran up to me and pointed, laughing. A child wearing my mother's face.

The procession and grim display went on and on, the eyes in every face dull as smudged glass, nothing to be gleaned from the waxen expressions. Whatever lay below the surface was well beyond my perusal, but in the thinking, I knew there was nothing to be perused.

This was artifice, nothing more.

No reason to struggle, they dragged me onward, flesh torn from my feet and I did not care. Dragged me toward a building that might be a police station or a music club or even Skull Island. Could be anything.

Anywhere.

Anywhere my brain made it.

Anywhere *our* brains made it.

I wish, somehow, that I could shape things to find my own escape.

There had to be a way.

There had to be a way *out*.

But before that is found, I find myself in a tiny room, walls black, painted with unmoving shadows, one light, a man-made sun, beating down on me, melting me but not, but could I melt? Was that an option here? The force of the beam was a beacon of suffocating oppression incinerating all focus.

"Do you know why you are here," asked the cop who looked like Frank, this masquerade most amusing in a rather ironic way, what with Frank's run-ins with the police over the years, his lack of respect for authority figures. Even Average Joe's principal foil, Detective Bob, was a sterling example of this attitude, a seat-of-the-pants detective who often sidestepped the rules, much to the eye-rolling or head-turning chagrin of the authorities, who gave him slack because he got the work done...well, except for apprehending Average Joe.

One of the faces in the crowd could have been cut from Frank's description of Detective Bob.

"Did I ever tell you the one about the writer who lost his way onto the revelations that might save a friend or two, or himself?" Izzy said.

"Want a drink, Derek?" Frank said, calling me by name this time, a bottle of Jack Daniels uncapped and awaiting consumption.

"Don't mind if I do." Frank again, big swig, downing a third of the liquid in one gulp, as if it was water.

As the light burned into my corneas, irises, retinas, sliding languidly back along membranes and into the brain, burning there, maybe singeing holes within the hemispheres, the door swung open. Another cop sauntered in, but no, not another cop, not exactly. It was Aleister, of course. Why would I have expected anybody else?

"Hiya, chief," said the cop who looked like Izzy. Aleister swatted him hard on the back of the head. Izzy, oblivious. A Cheshire cat on acid smile is smeared across his face.

His waxen face. As with everything here, it is the culmination of Madame Tussaud's wet dream.

He starts to melt.

Aleister leaned forward and asked, "Where's Alethea?" I notice his badge. It actually said "Nobody" on the badge. No numbers, no name. Nobody.

I glanced at Frank's badge: "Help me, Derek."

And Izzy's badge, which is not a badge anymore, it is a pink flower with a face painted on it. As I stare at it, it spits at me. Water squirts from the center. It feels good, almost soothing, amidst the crematorium heat of the interrogation lamp.

I think crematorium, as if that has significance. As if death is near, perhaps? But who's death?

Pieces pulled together. Izzy continued to melt, his face elongating, the smile stretched to a snapping point. A clown's greasepaint mask, pooling in his collar. Frank began to melt as well, cellulite bubbling along his cheeks, his hair pasty and dripping. I shook my head, tears of frustration hot on my cheeks, wondering if I am melting too, somehow knowing I am not, yet the incapacitation of the situation—this reality, the other reality, all of the realities that I have been burdened with over the last few days—is too much, too damned much, and it all feels hopeless—

("Derek.")

—It all grinds like the machinery of something made to grind hope and bones and reality and perception and brains and—

("Derek, come back to me.")

—Aleister leaned closer and I could smell the woodsy musk of the forest on his breath, the first thing in this reality that feels right, because it is not of this reality. And in feeling right, I can't say it is comforting. I feel everything, so it is real. But this has nothing to do with reality. This is the result of an unwavering curiosity that nature, specifically that place in the forest, has incorporated as necessary within the context of its survival.

This is nature emboldened with the power of something we would consider as godlike, but unlike many humans, nature is not restricted to the weaknesses that belief in an unknown entity entails.

Nature is, nothing more. Its aspirations are simple. It is a child forever.

Aleister, removing his cap, the translucent wax covering his head dripping away to reveal the diseased, porous brain within, beetles scurrying in and out of the labyrinth of tunnels, asked, "Where's Alethea, Derek?"—

("Derek, wake up.")

—and it behooves me to say, "She's over *there*," no specific designation of where "there" is, just the statement without evidence.

Aleister said, "I need to help her," and I am made to understand that, somehow, he means her no harm. This madman means her no harm. What of his warped, mangled memories? Well, yes, *he is a madman*, but somewhere within, a nub of empathy is present. And there was that moment I intuited his love for her, so pure.

Nonetheless, I have no idea where "over there" is, it's just a voice—

("Derek.")

—*in my head*.

"She's in here," I said, pointing to my head, as if it is a bus or plane that will take us to wherever she is *over there*, but the madness of this does not deter Aleister—

("Derek, c'mon, Derek...")

(A sense of being shook, of hands on my shoulders.)

—who said to me, "Well, then," pulling the arm of the interrogation lamp toward my face, it having already melted Frank and Izzy to puddles of oily flesh at our feet, though making out that much is only a perceptual assumption.

He said, "You should probably quit fuckin' around in your head here and get back to her *over there*..."

("Derek. You have to wake up now. It's all too weird and *you are no longer a tree*.")

The light moves closer, burning bright as the sun but without the sun's blinding beauty, just blinding me unmercifully.

Aleister slid his gun from its holster and raised it to my head, and said, "Maybe she just needs a way out, y'think?"

("Okay, Derek. G-Get the point?" *Aleister's* voice, from *over there*...)

Aleister, from here, "Maybe we just need a way out..."

(...over there: *inside my head*.)

("De—")

I gasp, groan, eyes aching with the light, but this is the beautiful burn, this is the burn that melts everything around me from that other place and I am over there, which is now here, and here is the forest and a halo of sunlight surrounds the figure above me, her head, and *her face*. Alethea.

"Derek. We have to get out of here. Now."

Otherside

"You have confused the true and the real."
        —George Stanley/In conversation, via Samuel R. Delany's
epigraph for *Dhalgren*

21: Aleister in the Flesh

I'm dazed and confused, Robert Plant's piercing wail briefly scratching at my thoughts as my hands clawed at dirt; dirt that sifts through my fingers. It feels good, this concentrated revelry, but Alethea is swift to break the spell.

"Derek. I cannot impress upon you enough to get up, let's go. Now!"

Alethea looked so beautiful I wanted to kiss her all over her face, lick her like a happy puppy greeting its owner after too long away. But the look in her eyes was rimmed red and bloodshot streaked like many dying shooting stars. Her pupils were large as quarters, maybe half dollars, and she's pulling on me and I'm still flimsy, my muscles refusing to react until I see something reflect in her glossy eyes, something to make me sober.

"Can't stay here. Must leave. G-Go now..." Aleister or Alexander or whoever (Nobody) leaned over my shoulder and said this, leaned too close, tics riding the flesh under the skin of his face. Alethea doesn't seem the least bit startled, but I jump and am up, ready for anything, to sprout wings or simply rocket into the sky, join the dying shooting stars in her eyes. *Anything was possible.*

"Alethea, he's really here." I grip her bicep, feeling the tensed muscle.

"Yes, I know, Derek. When I was the ivy at the base of you when you were the tree, I sensed everything and sensed deeper and even saw some of what he saw when he was stepping on me."

I turned to look at her and she nodded her head and there was really no reason to get into the absurdity of it all. Just before I'd awakened in the city, I had noticed ivy wrapped around my base, moving, wanting to protect me, I'd thought. There was no reason to believe that it was not her, Alethea. Under the circumstances, it made sense.

I was not alone in my experience.

"We need to go, Derek. Asap if not sooner."

"What's the hurry?" I said, standing on my own two legs again, hoping that these were actually my legs and not another dream manifestation made temporarily real.

"We have to get back to Frank. He needs our help."

"How do you know this?"

"You really want an answer for that question that's going to make sense?" She smirked, the perfect reflection of events in motion.

"What about him? He's killed people, Alethea."

She took my hand and we started to leave, and like that happy puppy I thought I wanted to be a minute ago, Aleister nipped at our heels, his whole body a collection of spasmodic twitches. His eyes were chameleon-like as they tried to look in front and around, upside down and over there, which was now here.

I reiterated: "He's killed people. He's crazy."

"I know he's killed people. I know he's crazy."

We had both mentioned Aleister's depleted mental capacities aloud, but in glancing back at him, it didn't matter. It wasn't a secret to him. But he knew of something more as well.

"I told you I sensed that," she continued. "But he wouldn't have done anything if he hadn't felt the necessity to get to me. He knew of my danger. Our danger, I guess. The only way for him to escape was to kill those people. That was how *his* logic made it right, worked it out. He will eventually have to pay for those consequences, but right now..."

Too much odd and conflicting input, so instinct took over, human instinct, not something culled from the dark past with misread intentions, but something of familiarity, of function, as we walked fast and faster, almost a jog, and the sudden realization that we were both naked, and I thought of Aleister's clothes, scavenged from his victim on the road.

"Where are our clothes?"

"Somewhere back there, I'm sure," she said, glancing behind us. "I don't think you want to go back and get them, do you?"

"No, no." I shook my head, unable to suppress my smile, much as if I'd just had a hit of a joint, or wandered into the smoke.

"What happened?" I asked, to nobody in particular, just my inner thoughts slipping through amidst events most oblique.

"As far as I can make it out, the forest is a conscious thing."

"Yes, conscious, not evil as suggested by my first impressions, but conscious, aware."

"And primal in its motivations. It casts influence as one would a net."

"It takes what it needs to shape something of substance out of the mental debris of those who come within the perimeters of its net of influence."

We stopped, Aleister bumping into us, then stepping back, head tilted, curious. Alethea and I were so in sync on this it was as if I was talking to myself.

She broke the silence, questioning: "What do you make of it all, then? What was it like to be a tree?"

"It was not bad being a tree," I said, smiling, again shaking my head, this time at the impossibility of it all, aware in my own way the realm of impossibilities was no longer a valid perspective in my life. *Anything was damn well possible.* "It wasn't a bad thing, an evil thing." A pause before aligning the truth. "Actually, it was the most alive I have ever felt."

"Yes," Alethea said, as we commenced walking, much to Aleister's obvious contentment, bopping along behind us. "I felt strangely alive in my vine-like state as well. It seems the forest took the tree and vines as major focuses of the beings we are, maybe as something it could relate to. Somehow seeing or sensing the tattoos on our bodies, and shaping the tree and vine from our flesh. Maybe it was easier than digging inside our heads, maybe—"

"Completely ridiculous."

"I agree, and I'm the one who believes in magic. I need a new hobby."

"I have to help Alethea," Aleister said.

"How do you have to help her, Aleister?"

His face scrunched like a discarded paper bag, a two-point slam dunk into the garbage container.

"Have to help her. To pull her out. Out of...that place. Before it took her. Took her for good. Like your friend...he has bad brain. It likes b-bad brain. Easier to digest." His words spat out as short, sharp jabs.

I had to stop my progress again, was about to speak when Alethea interjected, "I think he might know that because he's always been very sensitive to people's energies, auras, whatever you like to call it, even more so than I like to think I am. He was always trying to protect me, but lost his way because the circumstances of his life were too much to deal with. He didn't choose the best career to alleviate the empathic influx—"

"Empathic influx? He's murdered. How can there be any empathy involved in murder?"

"He wasn't always"—she paused, thinking, weighing the appropriate answer, understanding its legitimacy—"*broken*. His purpose with the band was to open people's minds. But he could never control it, what he felt. And he never understood it, as far as I can tell. Never understood what it did to him."

"Are we talking telepathy? This sounds like Cronenberg's *Scanners* brought to life." I felt as if my head would explode.

"Kind of. More like a deep intuition. Telepathy is science fiction."

"This whole thing is science fiction, horror, whatever—"

"Not whatever. Science fiction, horror, yes; however you want to designate it. I think Aleister may be correct in stating that Frank has somehow been a trigger for negativity within this place—"

"Well, yeah. At this point it's rather obvious, what with Average Joe's interaction with me when I was a tree." I couldn't help laughing now, the illogicality overwhelming me. "It doesn't take deep intuition to make sense of that, even if it is all nonsense."

"And with the forest having consciousness, and its roots, as a part of nature, being the primal blueprints from birth, the birth of the earth. Damn!" Alethea joined me as we laughed, the ludicrous manifesto we laid out, red-lined and in need of a re-write, or possibly the strike of a match. She put both hands on her head as if trying to hold it together. I took her left hand again and squeezed hard.

"I just can't wrap my brain around it. I believe in things both mystical and magical, or at least try to, but right now, I don't want anything to do with either."

"I know," I said, moving back to the here and now and away from our deflating speculations. "But if Frank is somehow responsible, the primary source that the forest has been feeding on, even though much of what I experienced as a tree was culled from my thoughts, memories and such, then what can we do?"

"I'd say" — she looked at me, then herself, then me again — "get some clothes and get over there, talk to him. See what we can gauge from that. Realistically, I'd say we're probably going to have to drag him away, whether he wants to leave or not. I should have some sweats that will work for you."

"What about him?" Nodding in Aleister's direction.

"I'm not sure. I know there is more for him, but cannot really guess what his part in all of this is. Yet. I'm sure we will find out soon enough."

We left the density of the trees, both Frank's and Alethea's houses in view.

"Not good. Not good," Aleister said, roughly grabbing Alethea's arm.

"Not good, maybe, but we need to see what we can do to help Frank, maybe stop the snowballing madness," Alethea said, gently pulling Aleister's hand from her wrist, yet still holding onto it, the look in his eyes one of stark fear.

It set me on edge.

We'd left the back door open to Alethea's house as that was the door we had exited what seemed a lifetime ago. Upon entering, Alethea rushed to her bedroom; I got to take in her body again, as it was now, this fit woman, but also remembered her body as Aleister had remembered it. Even amidst the conflicting input, I realized I was showing signs of life in places that should remain composed, at least under the present conditions.

"Might want to put that in here," Alethea said.

"Yeah, well…"

I thought about keeping it to myself, then thought, what was the use?

"In his head, while I was there, I saw you and him having sex, and these images were not complimentary." For lack of a better word. Me, the writer, again at a loss for words. I glanced toward Aleister perched at the window, peering at Frank's house. "If he is so intuitively sensitive, those images seemed quite contradictory."

Alethea considered this and said, "We were never lovers, never intimate in any way besides ideas and music."

"But your body...it was you, yet..."

"He may have seen me naked, the chaos of rock 'n' roll touring. Of rushing from here to there and such. I'm sure he did." The lines on her forehead creased: remembrance. "Well, he was with me for much of the tattoo work, often holding my hand, being supportive. I can say there was a real connection during this process, something of empathy. He had even teared up and seemed in general discomfort the whole time. Odd, I'd not thought of that in years."

"But it was more as if he didn't like you, the brute force of it."

"Maybe that experience, the harsh intensity of it, and our real connection during the process, has left some kind of negative residue. Maybe his sick brain has warped even that, his caring for me, into something grotesque. Again, we were close, maybe he wanted something more, but in all honesty he never acted on anything of that nature."

"That's what I thought. I must say, his brain is more than sick, it's a real mess." I stared at him. He hadn't moved at all, pensive, yet focused.

"I'm sure it is, from what little I had picked up. But I must say, I'm glad I didn't pick up on that. My reception was more clipped, scattered."

I slipped on the sweats and an old Dark Angel Asylum shirt that fit a little snug but beggars can't be choosers. My feet remained bare, but I had another pair of Converse sneakers at Frank's house. Being more presentable before entering was a good idea. All of us entering, including the recently escaped murderer with a good heart, or at least good intentions, might be a bit much, especially with Frank's mood recently, but that was the least of my worries.

"Looks better on you," I said, admiring Alethea's attire, similar to mine, but cut to fit.

"Shall we?" I said, taking her arm in mine, hesitantly walking toward the front door.

As we stepped onto the porch, I felt my heart stutter. Izzy's rental car was there.

"It's okay, Derek. So what if your friend Izzy is there as well. Might help us work things out, who knows?"

"How much of what transpired when I was a tree and you were a vine did you actually see through Aleister's eyes?"

"Not much. Glimpses, like I said. Mainly the last part when…"
She realized my concern.

I took a deep breath. Held it. Hoping when I went to shake Izzy's hand that it would not be an axe-arm.

"Well, here goes nothing…"

22: Red Alert

The door was unlocked, as I expected. When Frank and I had gone out to get some food the day I arrived, I'd noticed he had shut the door without locking it. He said this was the kind of place where people didn't find it necessary to lock their doors; the kind of place where people always felt safe. I remember thinking in San Francisco I had an array of locks, deadbolts, and occasionally propped a chair against the door, my quest for security necessary for my relaxation; my quest to feel safe.

I hadn't really felt safe the whole time I'd been here, and right now safety seemed about as farfetched as winning the lottery.

Since we already had enough to deal with trying to convince Frank into leaving, along with the possibility of physically maneuvering him if talk didn't do the trick, Alethea and I realized Aleister's presence might actually create undue concern. Especially since Frank knew of Aleister's escape, utilizing the information as a springboard for the resurrection of Average Joe. Aleister's presence was a distraction we didn't need to deal with. It was enough of a distraction to me, even if I believed what Alethea had said about his being here. Strangest white knight I'd ever imagined.

We entered to laughter from above, from Frank's room.

I glanced at the wood stove. No changes since "Bradford" had taken form, which, now that I think about it, was about the time things went well off the deep end and into the crapper.

Trepidation raced rat-like up my spine and clawed at my cerebral cortex as I went to the sofa and slipped on my Converse sneakers, which sat in front of it.

"Maybe we should leave," Alethea said, her courage deflated.

She must have felt the same spine-rattling chill.

"No, we have to face this." I said. I thought of the cop who looked like Frank, and his badge: "Help me, Derek."

Though Frank had had a hand in the shaping of this madness, in what the forest had latched onto, if my perceptions were correct (a debatable proposition at best) he knew he was in deep and needed a life preserver or, at least, help.

"Derek!"

Izzy, from atop the stairs. With a mix of amusement and apprehension I watched him jog down the stairs, looking fit, but with the appropriate signs of age: salt and pepper sideburns, prominent crows' feet. These things were not evident on the previous incarnation of Izzy that I had seen.

He reached the floor with a bounce in his step and gave me a bear hug. I was hesitant, but hugged back.

This seemed like Izzy, if Izzy had aged eight years and still had his childlike glee. Like the wood stove, he seemed more complete now, the finished version.

Frank followed Izzy down the stairs, a bit of a spring in his step as well. The edges of his features still seemed carved out of something gloomy, but the smile he wore was trying to chip the gloom away.

Maybe everything would be okay. Seemed impossible, but here we were, what seemed like reality not just taking shape but in full form and not hesitant to stick around.

I knew I was kidding myself, hoping for the best when, with Izzy's refinement, it was obvious reality was not only off the deep end and in the crapper, but shamelessly doing the backstroke as well.

"Where've you been, Derek?" Izzy said. He broadened the silly putty of his face, his voice shifting, acclimating to the overwrought, positive cadences of TV psychologist Dr. Phil, as grafted onto the glazed, about to explode glare of the late stand-up comedian, Sam Kinison, the two major influences in the creation of his *Psychobabble* alter-ego, Leonard Thumley. "Talk to Dr. Thumley about your problems, Derek. Remember, you cannot change what you do not acknowledge," he said.

Alethea's grip on my hand tightened. Izzy's look, a spot-on, eyebrows arched Dr. Phil impersonation to match the voice, was accentuated by what could only be described as Average Joe's prodding sneer.

Worse yet, his eyes registered as empty in a way that corresponded with Frank's description of Average Joe: "…a blank slate in which good and evil and right and wrong jogged beside other words like death and love and rose and elephant with equal triviality."

Or possibly like the eyes of those in the city I had visited. Coals again, without even the pretext of ever being lit.

Alethea took the lead, shifting the dynamics as best as possible. "Hello. My name is Alethea. Derek's told me so much about you." I hadn't told her that much, but she played it right, as Dr. Phil and Average Joe disintegrated. Izzy broke into laughter.

"If he told you anything, you'd better call the authorities, dear," he said, extending his hand to her as if touching it was a dare, then turning to me, he said, "Maybe call the police, eh, Derek?"

I thought of the city much like mine again, but not, and of the police all wearing familiar faces. I wondered if Alethea had any inkling to the devious intent the remark suggested. It seemed not, though her grip of my hand remained resolute. Then again, it might have been to borrow my strength as she reached her right hand toward his.

As they touched I felt a profound vacancy of self, similar to the annihilation of identity that Aleister so wanted to assimilate, yet here it was complete. It felt like sentient electricity, like a raging forest fire singeing the blackened byways of neurons in full-on retreat mode. "Red Alert" flashed in my brain.

This interpretation was brief, as if whatever evil was present was aware of possible detection, and attempted to shield its presence. With the knowledge that evil was present, not just consciousness, but evil, the one human aspect that nature could truly understand, relishing the abandonment of human wiles amidst the lurid pull of instinct, I understood that we were in the presence of something beyond compare when it came to the personification of evil. We were in the presence of Average Joe,

Frank's premier creation, not Izzy. In Frank's mind, Izzy was a building block in the formation of Average Joe, nothing more. In Frank's mind, perhaps Average Joe was even more real than Izzy.

I felt confident that the real Izzy was still married and living in Germany.

After she released his hand, Alethea seemed none the worse for wear. She showed no signs of what I had felt, nothing beyond the discomfort of the situation at hand.

"When did you get here, Izzy?" I decided not to let on that I had sensed anything. I had the feeling that it wouldn't be long before it all flipped, so might as well plant my feet solidly on the ground to brace myself for whatever the flipping would unveil.

"You know when, don'tcha remember?" He looked at me quizzically, as if I was the one with the problem. I remembered his initial question when he made it down the stairs: "Where've you been, Derek?" not "How've you been?"

Yet the salt and pepper sideburns, the crows' feet digging in, that's not who (or what) I saw last night. This version of Izzy still thought as the initial version from our original encounter here. It either knew and was denying it, or knew and was egotistical enough to think it could just bypass the obvious and move on to whatever was next.

Which, of course, made little sense. Ego? Then again, this place, this forest, *this nature*, might just have the confidence to think it could get away with anything, no matter the reality that intruded on its games. Because its reality was of a different structure than my reality. Because its reality was only viable as fantasy fulfillment.

Because the snapping of a twig under heavy snowfall and the creation of a monster with an axe for a hand were of equal veracity within its tainted realm.

I remembered what Alethea had said about characters in novels, how you can get close, but the real, the flesh, the idiosyncrasies and vitality, were beyond the reach of mere words. This place was doing a pretty good job of filling in the cracks, yet because of the constant reevaluation of mental input, the lie was made more obvious. It had to have dug deep into my brain to perceive my impressions, while talking to the original version of

Izzy. Hence, the aging done today, to fit what I thought Izzy should look like at this point, as opposed to the original input as assembled from my memory files. Add to the mix Frank's Izzy connection to Average Joe, and the forest was blissfully overburdened with the bounty of impressions pertaining to this one person, this one character.

"Are you ready for everything, Derek? Are you ready to give in and play with fire?" Frank said this as he moved next to Izzy...or Average Joe, or at least the seeds of Average Joe. Perhaps there was a battle raging in Frank's head, between Izzy and Average Joe, and this version was the result, one whose reliability was fickle, ever-shifting.

Izzy sweated profusely, wiping his face. With every wipe, the wrinkles smoothed out. He brushed his hair back with both hands, the span reaching his sideburns and, with the motion, the salt and pepper deepened in tones to Izzy's more natural dark brown.

From the front door behind us, Aleister yelled, "Leave now. He is not who he is. He is the force. The sh-shaping force. The other one is the—"

23: The Big Picture

Feedback squealed across the ceiling, an electric tomcat on midnight prowl, howling as it raced across the roof. The sound ricocheted back and Aleister grabbed his head as if it would explode, eyelids clenched, stumbling outside amidst the sonic verification of the pandemonium within.

I turned to Frank and said, "You asked me for help, Frank," and shoved Izzy backwards. Alethea took a preparatory stance, ready to fight.

"How can I help?"

A roll call of emotions played out on his face. Sadness, futility, desperation, resignation, defeat, and even a rebellious bud of acceptance of the challenge at hand, whatever challenge that might be.

I grabbed him, ready to drag him away, expecting that would be the only way to give him a chance to escape the forces here and what those forces had helped create in the name of his imagination.

Izzy regained his composure, a look of perplexed shock on his face, though he followed up with one of his usual lines. "What? You don't love me anymore?" A line that Frank had purloined from Izzy and given to Average Joe, the duality on display before me.

The probability that this was Average Joe, the fiction in the flesh, curdled my headspace. Yet the irrationality confirmed by pushing him, feeling the weight of the fantasy made real, this kind of deception was beyond my ken, but obviously within the realm of harsh truths that nature wanted to flaunt right now. He was a thing formed of corrupt imagination, perhaps birthed in that neon yellow bile as Doreen and Asia and the axe-armed version of him had previously been birthed. This truth filled my headspace without hesitation or denial.

Izzy reached for Alethea, but she was swift to slug him hard in the belly. He buckled over, laughing as he did, laughter laced with a raucous cruelty that I had always imagined Average Joe would sound like. Nothing like the laughter in the movies, the chameleon-like Christian Bale made remarkably plain, his seething cadences grinding like motorcycle rumble. This was more *real*, if that was possible. Alethea kicked him hard in the face as he grabbed at her legs. His laughter ceased. He spat blood and wiped his naked wrist across his mouth.

"That's not really all that funny, bitch!"

Feedback scrambled across the ceiling again, Aleister's torment lending the appropriate soundtrack to the madness at hand.

Another sound joined the feedback, a distant, whining chk-chk-chk, tightening of the screw in metal noise. The trees quivered in what could only be perceived as anticipation.

Frank casually lit a cigarette, as if he had all the time in the world. As if the fight playing out next to us was of minor consequence. He confirmed this thought when he said, "It all comes down to you and me, Derek. Whether I need your help or not, whether you can actually help me at this point, it all comes down to…"

We were interrupted as Alethea hit the hardwood floor with a bone cracking thump, the result of Average Joe having snatched her lethal leg mid-kick and twisted it with force.

"Little help, Derek," she said as she scooted crab-like away from Average Joe, favoring her left side as she did.

Frank took a deep drag, said, "You can help her if you want, but it doesn't really matter. You have yet to encompass the big picture, Cisco." He shrugged his shoulders, smoke seeping out of his lips, cobra-lethal snap as it did. I jumped.

Alethea was out the door, Average Joe hot on her heels, with obvious bad intentions in mind. I leaped full force onto his back, locking a full-nelson on him as I did, the force causing us to tumble onto the dirt outside.

With some kind of trickery only executed in dreams or highly choreographed martial arts fights in the movies, Average Joe flipped me over and twisted in ways that made his arms seem elastic, and, with astonishing grace, we had switched places. Now he had *me* in a full-nelson.

"Tit for tat, Derek, m'boy. I'll kill you too, but you have to wait your turn. She's pissed me off."

The corner of my eye wriggled with movement, Alethea twirling in a circle, the propeller-swing of a roundhouse kick in full-on knock-down mode, the weight of her muscular legs and the heel of her foot headed toward Average Joe's head, but he saw this as much as I saw it, and lifted me into the line of fire.

The impact dazed me, stars dancing a jig at the frayed edges of my vision, Alethea's, "Oh, shit," piggybacked by Average Joe's, "Shit yeah." I saw the blur of their bodies streaking across my sketchy vision, colors smudged and runny, but not as beautiful or as awe-inspiring as when I was a tree.

The smudges tumbled as one, this time near the logs, the axe, the hydraulic wood-splitter...

I heard the engine groan and knew it was going to get real messy any second now.

Black diamonds joined the stars as I stood up, wobbled, felt like a tree chopped through and awaiting the lumberjack's call of "Timber!"

I shook my head and stars and black diamonds scattered, shooting here and there, focus getting sharper by the second.

A sliver of feedback belched, but it seemed different, distant: there was no sign of Aleister. He claimed he was here to help, but with his absence, help how?

I saw Average Joe's arms wrapped around Alethea's body from behind, not a full-nelson, she was too squiggly to allow that body lock, but he still had a bear hug as they fell onto the hydraulic wood-splitter.

She was on top of him as he laid across its base, the splitting field, soon to be a killing field.

Average Joe leaned her toward the blade.

The sounds from the forest continued to mount in volume, a

slow, processional increase, as if carefully climbing up the rocky side of a mountain. Patient. Deliberate.

I sprinted, slid into the dirt next to the machine, and kicked at the lever. The engine sputtered and died.

The sounds hiccupped, grumbled in annoyance. The metallic timbres turned gummy as a throat gargling phlegm.

Snatching Alethea's hand, I realized this was not going to work. I would have to deal with Average Joe in order to get her free from this most dire of predicaments.

I grabbed at one of Average Joe's arms, his grip loosening. He realized he couldn't hold her and deal with my intrusion, so he reared back and bashed his head into hers; twice. The crack was painful to hear. She teetered and slumped, her consciousness cresting, on the verge of wiping out.

I hit Average Joe three times in the face, my fist tearing on his teeth as he started to laugh again. Apparently, the illogical sway of insanity snuffed out pain, or at least pushed pain into a place where it was barely acknowledged.

He was enjoying all of this.

Alethea staggered to her feet, drifting away, teetering still.

At that moment, everything froze, a jump cut to truths. As I pressed down on Average Joe and stared into his glacial eyes, he said in a voice the inflection of which mimicked Izzy's to perfection, "I thought you liked that I was a cut up, Derek. You know I can't help myself, like you. Contact high, what a goof, you always keep things in perspective. What you have to do to get through this is let go of *all* preconceived notions of reality here, in this place."

The moment thawed slightly, the voice changing again, this time catching me completely off guard. From Average Joe's mouth, Frank's voice: "You have yet to encompass the big picture, Cisco. What you know, or think you know, has no relevance here. Well" — the engine groaned again, me caught in the headlights—"unless you know how to use it."

My dominant position faltered, surprised to hear the engine. The wood-splitter groaned so loud in my ears it drowned out the forest's strange sounds, which had morphed into tones moistly stentorian and vocal again.

Average Joe hooked my side with his arm and leg, forcing my back to the blade. He had me, clearly had the advantage. We faced each other and it was plain that he didn't care what would happen to me, or him. The machine was revved and ready, the hydraulic insistence pulling the blade toward my spine.

In the instant before the wood-splitter blade would kiss my life goodbye, Alethea regained the wherewithal and strength to pull me up. But she paid the price as, out of nowhere, the blade of an axe ripped through the space between her and Average Joe. An axe head connected to his wrist. It skinned her arm, a clean incision from elbow to wrist. She screamed.

Average Joe shifted his weight, using the spontaneously generated axe-arm to prop himself up. With his free hand, he clawed at her, the pain rendering her momentarily immobile. But his efforts were stamped out as Aleister Blut landed atop him, a sudden, crushing impact that caused me to flinch, as if he had been dropped from the heavens. A gift from God? A condemnation? More likely an accomplice to chaos, that's all.

Their abrupt melding incapacitated Average Joe and, with compacting force, brought to fruition Frank's previously mentioned next step idea for bringing Average Joe back to life, utilizing the mind of a crazed rock star as vessel for further mayhem. From Aleister's mouth, Average Joe's voice said, "That's pretty fucked up, dude," before the feedback that had belched in the distance erupted into a white noise tsunami that surrounded us, the fangs of the noisy beast tearing at my eardrums. Aleister shrieked in pain and madness, *"No future here, not yours or mine,"* in his own voice, the last word stretched long as the wood-splitter blade bit into his side.

Another piece of the unreality puzzle had been revealed to me, though, with Average Joe's words having passed through Aleister's mouth. Obviously, despite what I saw, Aleister was as unreal as Average Joe, unless Average Joe had a talent for ventriloquism that Frank had never mentioned in the novels.

Aleister's death, or at least the finalization of his presence in this reality, came swiftly, as the feedback coughed and stuttered and, for a moment, the cacophonous noise assumed the guise of music, harmonious and beguiling in its beauty. It was as if everything that I had ever associated with aural beauty *in my life* had been summarized through this transitory snippet, the misplaced tranquility of this coda.

The forest had even assumed the role as mute witness to the proceedings, fallen silent amidst the sonic splendor.

Average Joe shattered the moment, mocking Aleister's lyrical prescience with his own insane interjections, gurgling, illegible utterances accompanied by exaggerated rolling eyes and a drooling smile. The blade pressed onward, locked into the relentless hydraulic routine, his bones crunching and splinting, blood spraying, the wood-splitter painted in gore, dripping and pungent. It lurched forward, intent on cutting all the way through him. What a cut-up, indeed.

I thought of what I had been shown and of how it corresponded here. What if the blade, this machine, had sentience? Would this action be the instinctual code that dictated its life? And, with that thought, who was I to believe otherwise?

These thoughts were trampled by Average Joe's unceasing laughter, even as the blade made its way through his body, viscera spilling forth in sticky, steaming clumps.

"Think there's a job for me in the circus, Derek? Better yet, y'think I'm the next Houdini, the next David Copperfield? I won't need an assistant. I can cut my own self in half." He shoved Aleister's maimed body aside and grabbed his legs, hoisting them atop the wood-splitter as the blade receded, a breath taken before the next slice 'n' dice effort, and, once again, the machine's hydraulic rhythms compressed with unrelenting force.

The blade split into the seam of him, straight up through the middle. Through muddled laughter, yet laughter nonetheless, he said, "Did I ever tell you the one about the…" but he paused before completion, tossing off his left leg, which had been severed all the way to the hip. "Skip it. Let's cut to the chase," he said, still laughing, the punch line sliced from this grisly climax, the blade pushing back and forth, his free hands assisting in his ghoulish self-annihilation. Two hands again, the axe-hand was gone, replaced by fingers that flexed, nails digging into the meat of him, clutching undefined chunks of himself and lobbing them at us.

"Fuck! Oh my…" A part of me wanted him to stop it, a part of me understood that this was not happening — *it wasn't real* — but the smells stained my nostrils and tongue, the sight made me wish for a darkness that brought only serenity.

I had the distinct feeling that if there was a bottom to this chaos, we were about to hit it, with no reassurance that we would get back up.

Alethea held her injured arm against her side and said, "C'mon. Let's go."

"Go where?" I said, not sure of what or where any of this would lead.

Average Joe continued to downsize himself, the stench tangy and rich with blood and hot oil as the machine's gears smoked and ground forth.

That's when I noticed Alethea's hand rubbing her arm, and the long, deep cut that I knew was there, healing with every caress.

Impossibly healing.

"No," I said, shaking my head, knowing now that, as I had been clued into before ("You have yet to encompass the *big picture*, Cisco"), this whole mess was not only a product of Frank's imagination, it had been colored by my unwilling contributions as well. My contributions might be lending a quirky angle to the madness that this place had latched onto with Frank, *but it was still madness*.

"C'mon, Derek," she said, tears streaming from her eyes. As far as I knew, this *version* of Alethea, probably a version channeled through the constructs of my own creation, Ashlyn Cage, was no closer to the real thing than the cackling maniac behind me, or Aleister.

Close but no cigar.

"C'mon, Derek," she said again, holding up her arm, a look of genuine shock as distilled by annoyance distorting her beautiful countenance. "What the fuck? I had sensed a purpose here, to help you to help Frank, but not…but not…"

Her features drew taut against the imagined skull beneath, her eyes losing vitality, as if they ever really had vitality. Had I been so blind as to not see this, to not see that she was not real? Had I been falling head over heels in love with a fantasy as channeled through my imagination, wanting to bring Ashlyn Cage front and center in the next novel, having researched Alethea to add meat to the character, the flesh and blood, history and aspirations, made real by this place?

The shock was as much hers as mine, because we both knew that it was all a masquerade, and in discarding the mask, she would be shown for what she was. Nothing but an elaborate fiction, the cruel fabrication and faux fulfillment of a dream.

"No," I said, feebly, the truth something I wanted to ignore. Not because I didn't want to "c'mon" with her any- and every- where, but because it made that possibility null and void.

"Please, Derek," Alethea said. "Hold me." Tears glistened on her cheeks, but only those which had already fallen. No more followed, the grief a sham.

She knew exactly where she stood. She was a part of my imagination, somehow part of Frank's imagination as well, "...to help you to help Frank." That had to mean her purpose was something more than just to be my fantasy lover.

But she did not wish to leave quite yet.

"Hold me, Derek. Please."

I approached her, the wood-splitter grunting with mechanized exhaustion, Average Joe laughing, but even the vindication with which he had formerly expressed his joy was fading fast.

I took her hand, a hand as real as anything I had ever touched with my fingers, and pulled her close to me, wanting to meld as one again, to know that experience again, with her, no matter the legitimacy of the experience.

It was something to be cherished forever.

She looked in my eyes, but already I could see the traces of her dissolving. She kissed me on the cheek as I pulled her into a strong embrace, wanting to express so much but the expression was unnecessary.

She knew. After all, she was a part of my imagination, no matter the flesh forged in *this* reality.

She looked at me again, and the dissolving traces stabilized.

She held firm and brushed her lustrous lips against mine. The sensation tantalized like nothing I had ever experienced before, and at that instant I knew we were one in a way that defied everything I had perceived here, or would ever understand again.

I felt the mass of her "poof" as a dandelion would when the magic of warm breath would kiss it. Alethea, my fantasy version of Alethea, was reduced to pollen, seeds.

Nothing.

She was so real, but she was not real at all. My inclination was to scream out her name for the loss, but how could I justify that in my head? It sank back within me, the grief forever a part of me.

I glanced behind me as Average Joe continued his slice 'n' dice nonsense. His laughter had abated since he'd cut his face in half, yet the pieces that remained somehow functional continued with the depressing exercise.

"It all comes down to us, Derek," Frank said, from his back porch, seeming anxious. A balloon being blown up past capacity, about to burst.

"You wanted my help. Let's go, get away from here. We need to leave, my friend. Things happening here should not be allowed to happen. Your only chance is to leave with me, now."

My words were dry, reality still on the edge but slapping me hard in the face with Alethea's loss. I could still smell her, taste her.

"I want your help, but I…" he said, nodding toward the forest, "I need to go *out there*."

I approached him. "Why?"

I could see in his eyes the desire to go with me, but the desire was overshadowed by something he could not control. "I can't help it, Cisco. The forest, this place, won't have it any other way. And I can't have it any other way."

With that he broke into a surprisingly brisk sprint toward the forest, a scream of despair tagging along before the forest devoured the sound and he disappeared into the trees.

He was my friend and in order to get him back, I had only one option. I had to follow him.

He was right.

It would all come down to us, though I'm sure this place would have a say on the outcome. I would just have to find a way to alter things just enough to make a difference, and hopefully get Frank out of there…as well as myself.

24: The Death of Hope

Determination is one thing, idiocy another. Each took a hand and led me into the forest, toward the glade, that empty space bereft of conscience, but eagerly awaiting our showdown. Frank and I out there, with the knowledge I had now and not the ambiguities that had besieged my stay over the last few days. Since we were the dual protagonists of this macabre charade, it seemed likely that this carnival of craziness would continue.

Not for long, though. The end loomed ever closer, whether the forest realized it or not.

I wondered if the forest could pick up on this thought. Why not? I tried to clear my head of all wayward thoughts. I had to think of a way to get Frank out of there in one piece, no matter what it wanted, and away from here permanently. But how could I do this without this place deciphering whatever strategies I surmised and stomping on them before attainment?

I remembered, as Alethea had said, or as I had realized all along—after all, the inclusion of Alethea as my personal conduit, my analytic sounding board, was a self-made prophecy propagated by this place—the forest needed dark dreamers such as Frank, and, to a lesser degree, though no less vital, me. The forest fed on these things.

I had to figure out a way to take what the forest wanted and bend it to my ultimate goal, all while under cover of false pretenses.

I was at a loss. I could really use Frank's more concise, disciplined understanding of deception right about now.

As I made my way deeper into the forest, I heard the hum of guitars at rest, awaiting the bashing power chord, or simply the knob-twisting, decibel enhancing gift of feedback, again. It was the tattered remnants of Aleister Blut that the forest had treasured so much. His noise-riddled mind. It was the tattered remnants that remained, no matter Aleister's vacancy.

Or possibly it was the seeds of my own aural assimilation of all that had come to me over the last day. After all, the materialization of Aleister, like Alethea and Izzy and Average Joe (and Frank—this had to be considered), was a construct of all the information I had ever digested about him, as expanded on by my acuity and imagination.

Laughter reverberated inside me. My laughter, approaching delirium.

I stopped for a moment, closed my eyes, and thought of Alethea.

I felt her near, smelled her fragrance, could taste her again in my mouth and swished it around, wishing I could bathe in the saliva, the nectar of the gods.

When I opened my eyes, I was still alone.

Another squeal rippled below my feet. I actually saw the ground roll as a wave, as it had done the previous evening. The rolling tore a path through its center, right before me. The foliage and stumps and a couple of trees parted as I or Disney, my impressions manipulated via the memory of some forgotten but presently exhumed reel of animation, had imagined the Red Sea had parted for Moses, but the path laid out here glimmered blindingly. A yellow brick road.

I was never a fan of *The Wizard of Oz*. Frank liked it, though.

The bricks sparkled, more from beneath than above, as the trees that I passed clustered in large groups, blocking out the sun.

I walked along that path, the gold bricks my red carpet jaunt into madness, when I saw Frank. He paced in a small circle, shoulders slumped, cigarette squeezed tight between his lips.

I stopped in front of him, the surroundings almost serene, the proverbial calm before the storm, I thought; better yet, the weird before the weirder.

The ground beneath my feet was dirt again, the golden yellow bricks gone. Fool's gold, teasing me.

I stood in front of him, in the middle of that now familiar glade. After a time as Frank smoked the cigarette, red tip racing to the end with every deep inhalation, he looked up at me.

"So, what do we do, Pancho?" I said as I put my hand on his shoulder. He reached across with his free hand, the one not about to be burned by ash, and squeezed it. He dropped the butt of the cigarette and stamped it out, his final smoky exhalation, companion to a sigh.

"I-I wanted your help, but didn't know how to go about it, Derek."

The trees shook violently, no noticeable escalation of wind in the shaking.

"It's been so long, but I need to rest."

"What are you talking about? The forest, this place, has messed with us. Don't know how, but it has. But we've always come out ahead when things get rough, so why stop now?"

I tried to look and seem confident, but was sure my eyes would tell a different story. It had been a wild ride.

The ground rumbled again. Though California was earthquake country, this sensation had nothing to do with the shifting of tectonic plates, or tapping a valve to alleviate pressure. This rumbling was autonomous, dictated by nature. The nature in this place. I had the distinct feeling that the forest in this desolate patch south of heaven and left of reality was not pleased with the vibe we were giving off, or perhaps was picking up on something I had yet to work out.

Feedback sizzled and simmered underneath it all like the amplified trespass of those damned beetles from the evening of Izzy's original appearance.

"You've always been a good friend, Derek. The best." He pulled a butcher knife from within his plaid shirt. My eyes grew large, my concern obvious.

"What? What are you doing?"

The low hum of amplifiers again, the forest engaged in our conversation, concentrating and curious. The hum droned, patient again. A static line, crisp and anxious.

"In order to make the character real, I had to experience what he experienced. I had to know what it was like to do those things."

He looked into my eyes and for that instant there was no doubt in my mind that he was Average Joe, not the made-up character, but the flesh incarnation. I knew that he had done everything that Average Joe had done, that he had done those horrendous things, yet I had to be wary of my perceptions because everything the last few days had shown me had toppled belief systems and even my own grasp of logic.

"You understand, don't you? It's what we did, experience things, experience life, to the fullest."

"No," I said, not wanting to believe it, but the look in his eyes, so unfamiliar to me, not the eyes I had known for so many years, let me know that these truths would bring sorrow. The rising tumult around me, the earth shaking—*this place knows it is true*—somehow confirmed that my best friend, Frank Harlan Marshall, had killed in the name of his art. That Frank Harlan Marshall had created a monster, Average Joe, but all he ever really had to do was look in the mirror.

He flipped the knife around, the blade pointed at him, the handle at me. "Spin the knife, take a life." I remembered that line from the second Average Joe novel, *Cut to the Chase*.

"I've had to live with the guilt for too long. I tried to justify it, but I killed people, innocent people, just to get it right for the novels. The character. And this place"—nodding to the forest around us, the feedback whine mounting, shaking the shrubbery, shaking my bones and the branches above—"this place enjoys the bloodshed, the darkside, and will not allow me to leave. It will never allow me to leave. Ever." He held the knife up to me, insistent now. *Take it!*

I thought, with what he had claimed to have done (*confessed*), there would never be any way he could leave his own mental prison, the wilderness within.

I took the knife. It felt weighty but cold; indifferent, I thought, giving it sentience, an abstraction extrapolated in my head. A knife did not care who or what it cut into, that was what it was for. Its purpose. Its instinct.

I laughed, couldn't hold it in, the first exclamation point for my sanity.

The ground below me groped at my feet, the dirt scaling the sides of my shoes.

The instant my fingers wrapped around the handle, my grip firm, the forest broke into a din of hoary noise, an extravagant collection of small sounds made large—the few insects and birds that still trespassed here—and impossible sounds as fact.

Impossible? I laughed again, the second exclamation point to my swiftly vacating sanity.

I was engulfed in acidic epithets flung by nature's tongue, the mysterious language of wood and leaf, of wind that whispers sweet nothings and the alluring shimmer of deceptive charms here, in this place, this obscene forest.

It was anxious for *real* blood to be spilled in its presence.

I loosened my grip. The sounds swirled, simmered. My breath came back to me.

"Be strong, my friend. I've done wrong. I can never leave this place. But that doesn't matter. The guilt, something I had for so long not allowed purchase in my head, is worse than any sentence this place could distribute. But it finds pleasure in my grief and that much I cannot endure."

With that, a hiccup of noise that left a parched tickle in the back of my throat, a bitter taste on my tongue.

My grip tightened again. I didn't know if I had it in me to do what he wanted. I didn't know if I could do it under any circumstances. I was not judge and jury. I had known him for a lifetime and even if he had been a mess, he had also been a friend, a partner in my life's journey.

I didn't even know if I believed him, the possibility that this confession was a product of this place's wishes and avaricious instinct to have me join fully in the tenebrous realm of Frank's mind.

I didn't want to believe because he was my friend.

"Remember when we lost touch with Izzy? How we said it was like he fell off the edge of the earth? That's because they never found his body. Him and his wife, Jesse."

I didn't want to believe my friend was a murderer. But I could see no hint of a lie, and I had seen Frank lie many times to other people. There were none of the tell-tale signs. I wanted there to be some. I really wanted there to be some.

"You have to kill me, Derek. It's the only way either of us will leave this place. Without my memories, the forest will flounder, and you will leave, and leave all memories of this place here as well. Because, though your stories may be dark, there is always hope."

"Christ, Frank. You killed people? You killed Izzy?"

Frank smiled and something sinister skulked behind those eyes. He was remembering, and the memories brought him happiness. Despite the so-called guilt, he relished them.

I wondered if this place understood what he was saying, though in actuality, I knew it had to know. But it also wanted my full involvement in a murder here, now, to feed its atavistic needs. I expected that, my participation or not, the forest would not let me leave anyway.

What exactly was Frank's ploy? Was he so selfish as to eradicate his guilt while trapping me here to tend to this place's needs thereafter?

The forest floor started to boil, that sickly neon yellow fluid oozing from many points around me.

"You're going to have to kill me; otherwise my mind will find ways to add you to the death list." Spoken not as a threat, but as fact.

A dozen or more blotches across the twigs and dirt swiftly took form, axe-arms pulling the bodies out of the muck, the bodies coated and dripping and I realized that it was not the memory that made him smile, it was Frank finding the only way out of this mess for both of us.

He knew I would never be able to kill him, no matter his confession, counterfeit or not, but he was onto something here, creating something of immense, appalling wonder.

"If you did these things, why couldn't you just kill yourself instead of leaving this in my hands?" I had to drag it out until it was all made clear to me.

A snicker from Frank. Tiny, knowing.

The noise grew rabid, frothing at my eardrums, nipping at all thought.

Five of the bodies stood outside of the muck, stretching, flexing axe-arms, ready to kill, no faces, nothing to distinguish themselves from each other or anybody else.

An army of Average Joes.

Frank smiled again, the sinister edge receding, and said, "Distractions, Cisco," and with a whoosh not unlike Alethea's evaporative sayonara, *his image* was blown into thousands of pieces that flitted to the forest floor, only to evaporate upon touching the roiling soil.

The many faceless monsters followed suit, assisted by the turbulence triggered by the rage of the trees. The wind swooped down to batter my body, my face, the dirt and pollen and insects and even animals caught in the swell of its hot breath swirling around me, a tornado sculpted from despair, something nature, this place, had never experienced on this level and could never truly understand.

I yelled, "Stop," and the commotion ceased instantly. I still had a say on some level, probably because the forest's anger, anguish, and confusion weakened it.

I stood there, pensive, breath like fire scorching my lungs, knowing what I knew.

I flashed on something Frank had said: "…though your stories may be dark, there is always hope."

No, my friend. There was not always hope.

So, what did I really know?

What I knew was this. Frank needed me here to help him escape from the psychological clutches of this place, and his own mind. I'd only hoped it was the forest from which he was trying to escape. But, despite the fact that the Frank I had conversed with in the forest was only an image, there was something within the sadness that lent it veracity. This character was not a character, it had to be perfect in order to convince the forest; distract it. It was Frank, as close a creation as the real thing, because it *had* to be. I sniffed, snuffing out a laugh, the third exclamation point at the end of my sanity, thinking how Alethea would have to agree that this character was flawless, as close to human as possible.

So, what did I really know?

I knew there was not always hope. I was shown this as I stood there, the fire in my lungs extinguished by my decelerating breath, slowing down as I looked up and saw amidst the perplexing patchwork of spider webs a ghostly image dangling from above me, in the center of the forest, this bastard glade. I only glanced at it. I wasn't sure if tears were appropriate, but I let them come.

25: Confessions of a Dead Man

There was nothing mysterious or tainted in evil, unease or any like-minded emotion as I walked back to Frank's house. I took my time, as there was no hurry now, knowing what I knew.

When I made the back porch I had a moment where my inherent optimism, despite the confessions of Frank's doppelganger, ghost, demon or what-have-you in the forest, peeked through. But that curtain was closed upon entering.

As I stood in the center of the one large room downstairs, adjacent to the kitchen, I gazed up and saw Frank, the corporeal confirmation of the ghostly image that had dangled from the sky in the center of the forest.

The room reeked of death, something new *and real* added to my repertoire of experiences. The crude expulsion of Frank's bowels stained his pants. The dying heat of flesh as it invited rot, decay. The heady buzz of finality.

There were two notes on the table.

The first note laid out as the finale to a story—"Epilogue" was centered near the top of the first page—thanked me for my lifelong friendship, as well as attempted to explain what had transpired. "Your participation was necessary for my freedom. Your full immersion was necessary because I could never just state the facts and get it done. This place wouldn't let me. You had to get to know the true face of this place, of what I have been dealing with, in order to understand its motivations and what it was capable of doing. The participation of others was as much your involvement as mine. I teased this place with Izzy, and, more so, Average Joe. This place quite enjoyed Average Joe, had been enjoying him for months. I did this as much for distraction as anything else. Distraction so as to achieve my goals, but also distraction as shaped by my guilt. You brought Alethea and Aleister to the party. I helped lead them to the psychological rivers that flowed through me, you taught them how to drink, how to swim. But they were handicapped in the same way and couldn't state facts, could only hint at possibilities, maybe drop clues, whether they understood this or not. Whether understanding was even something they were capable of, I thought of them as puppets, nothing more. I tried to influence them, to keep them in check, not wanting them to let on to this place as to my plans. I'm sure you picked up on a lot of what was happening. I'm sorry about the obvious affection you had for Alethea, I'm sure you'll mull over that for a long time, but it was all necessary in order to get this thing wrapped up.

"This place would never have let me go. My mind would never have given me peace. This place was so locked into my personal darkness that I wasn't sure if I could mentally project myself long enough to finish the deal, to end my miserable existence, but with you on hand and a front row seat to bloodshed, I figured it might be enough of a distraction to let me do what needed to be done. I knew you would not kill me, that wasn't the point. That was up to me. It's what I needed to do, Cisco. It was what needed to be done."

Strangest thank you note I'd ever read.

Smart of him to construct it as part of a story, however loosely, so this place would not pick up on his true intentions, no matter the depth of the forest's prying.

The second note, more a stack of papers, detailed the deaths of those he had killed, including Izzy and Jesse. I skimmed these, confirming that he had told me the truth, and with this truth, had altered my thoughts of him forever. As much as he was my friend, maybe I'd never really known him.

No. Not maybe. I'd never really known him, a man I had qualified as my best friend, and now I had to wrap my brain around that. A lifetime of what? Lies? Some of the details, as I skimmed those pages, told of murders undertaken while we were hanging out together but, obviously, not always together, yet still while we were having our fun.

I called the police in Boone, explained the situation. They would be here as soon as possible.

"Could you please stay with the body, await the authorities?"

I agreed, depressurizing anyway, so why not? It was all nonsense at this point: Frank's suicide, his confession, Alethea, Average Joe, Aleister Blut, poor Izzy and Jesse, and the many others.

Nothing made sense and I feared nothing ever would. One doesn't spend a lifetime with somebody, close to somebody, and have this kind of information thrust upon them without repercussions. I would deal with it eventually. Right now, I just wanted to be far away from here.

I passed the wood stove, "Bradford" stenciled strong in the metal.

I stepped outside and inhaled deeply, washing away the odors from inside. I took in the house to my right, Alethea's house…in another frame of mind. I walked over to it and saw the front porch with its whittled wooden features and creatures, just as I had remembered them. I escorted a trickle of hope that, somehow, something here would make sense. I knocked and knocked again, with urgency. Peering into the window next to the door, I realized the place was vacant. I hit the door one more time, hard, expecting and receiving nothing but the hollow echo of defeat.

I thought the smile on one of the faces creased a little deeper.

Walking back toward Frank's house, not to step in, but to lean on my car, anxious for my own escape, I stared out to the forest and knew that all was calm now, not as the forest would like it, not this forest, this place, but for now and hopefully forever, it would remain helpless in its need to devour that negativity, and, apparently in Frank's case, the guilt, self-loathing, and scarred memories that it so loved. But nature lacked a conscience and I was sure that something or somebody weak, mad or mischievous would cross its path again.

So be it. Burn it down, I say, but that would fall on deaf ears. I could light a match now and really shake things up. Don't think I didn't consider it the best means of destroying or at least scaring what was out there. Maybe here I could be judge and jury, and executioner.

I lighted a match, having unconsciously picked one up while passing the wood stove, and smiled. Yes, that would be a good thing. But then again, what would be the use? Frank was dead, and Frank was not who I thought he was. What more would anything I did to this place matter? It had actually shown me Frank's true side.

I stared at the match, like the pit fire, the flame dancing, beautiful as it ate the wood, burning down, faster, faster, my fingers wanting to feel this. I let it nip and shook it out. I had control here. This place could no longer play games with my thoughts, and, anyway, the police cars and coroner had arrived, kicking up dirt and gravel behind me.

Epilogue: Ouroboros II

The bodies of Izzy and Jesse were found where Frank said he had buried them. Because of his timing and their lack of relatives, as well as Izzy's aloof demeanor, there was no brouhaha raised with their disappearance. I thought they had gone to Germany to live; those in Germany thought they had remained in America. Rumors occasionally surfaced that they had been spotted in other locales. After a year of no response to a few emails I had sent, as well as the disconnection of the only phone number I had for Izzy, I decided to let it be. I'd hoped they were happy, when in truth, they were already dead.

Other bodies were found where Frank had said he had disposed of them, though not all. The accumulation of years and varying methods of disposal made some impossible to confirm. Nonetheless, all told, twenty-seven unsolved missing persons' cases were solved.

I am still astounded at the total, and more so that the final tally included nine victims he had taken while we were on various vacations, our globe-trotting excursions no reason for him to stop his so-called research.

Aleister Blut's escape had been real, though at least the version that I had met had never taken on the personality of Average Joe, as Frank had planned to do with a new version of Average Joe loosely based on him. He had escaped, somehow vanished, without bloodshed. Wherever he was, I expected he still occupied his own lonely prison, in his head.

To my surprise, the house next door to Frank's was owned by Alethea, one of a couple she owned, the other being in New

Orleans, much as I had recollected the other version of Alethea had told me. She had filled me with truths, even though she was, ultimately, a lie, or perhaps my mind, as fueled by all of the information I had ingested about Alethea, had filled me with truths that shaped the lie. Apparently, she'd only lived in it sporadically since buying it a few years ago and not at all during the year that Frank had lived next door. She released a CD a few months after my ordeal, a CD dedicated to "magick, and the mystery of unknown places, where magick thrives, and the secrets of the earth frolic more freely, unbidden by the intrusion of humanity." I had every intention of getting in touch with her, but quelled that with the knowledge that it was best to leave it alone. She had her own life and beliefs and my allowing a fantasy version of her to influence the real world that I lived in was a preposterous concession. Anyway, I also knew that one of her key interests, as noted on her latest CD, would be a place I wanted never to explore again. I didn't even buy the CD upon release.

I went through many months of self-induced solitude. My whole life had been dismantled, turned to fiction in my head, as if I was a part of a story from which I wanted to disengage myself, yet because the story was as much Frank's story as it was mine, a complex interweaving of our lives, I couldn't let it all go. I couldn't justify what he had done, no sane person could. But he had been my friend and I couldn't let that go, either. Might skew some people's perceptions about me, but I couldn't really worry about other people's perceptions. I had my own brittle perceptions to deal with now. I felt much as I thought many people in a similar position would feel, much as Jeffrey Dahmer's parents had admitted in a documentary focusing on serial killers I had seen many years ago, about how they were hated or glared at with disdain because they loved him. What would you do if your son or daughter, father or mother, significant other or simply the person you *thought* you knew best in the world, turned out to be a serial killer? There might be anger, confusion, disgust…but hatred? Maybe, but I couldn't go there yet. I felt as if it would nullify my whole existence.

This was the bullshit that filled my lonely time, jousting with my personal demons and belief systems gone to weed. I couldn't say I even knew what true friendship was at this point.

Mostly what I felt was grief. I missed Frank Harlan Marshall. Our relationship was ingrained on my soul, or at least on the electrical impulses that drove me as a human being.

Part of my isolation had to do with my grieving. But most of it had to do with the media circus that followed. Since I was the only one there during Frank's finale, I was the only one with the story that our Too Much Information society wanted to hear or, more aptly, feed on. The vultures wanted to pick my brain, much as that place had picked our brains, but I wanted nothing to do with it, at least not at that time. The police got Frank's typed confession and detailed list of victims. I kept any deeper explanations and fantastical speculations to myself. I left the truth alone, because it was too unreal to comprehend.

Not surprisingly, Frank's book sales went through the roof after his death. The public seemed not to have a conscience as well.

I eventually got back into writing, though my writing had changed. There was no dismissing what had happened, so I incorporated it into a new novel, a kind of non-fiction fictionalization of my time with Frank, smudging the borders between the real and speculation, a popular conceit nowadays. My own *In Cold Blood*, with me closer to the murderer's black heart than Capote had ever imagined getting with his homicidal muses, Hickock and Smith.

The outline in my head for *Aftermath* was to divvy up alternating chapters: a primary chapter dealing with our friendship and the madcap adventures we had experienced, while a subordinate chapter of densely thought-out speculation would accompany it like an unwelcome guest whose candor dissipates the enjoyment of what had come before. Along with the speculation, when appropriate, note of a murder or murders would be added, statistics only: name of victim, where, when, and method of murder.

Almost immediately the outline was altered, lending the non-fiction and speculative observation chapters a serious dose of fiction and crude subtext. Frank's voice, as filtered through my head. Writing as Frank, those chapters followed my speculative forays, the unwelcome guest subverting everything to fit his own devious nature.

The outline followed suit thereafter, before the final draft found the book meshing the three viewpoints into one, where questions from the now fictionalized real experiences were answered immediately by my avatar, then debated by Frank, yet all within the constructs of a monologue as thought out by a never named narrator I could only define as "other." It had moved so far from my original idea, yet because I was a fiction writer, I felt that it made sense.

This was the story from which I had so wanted to disengage myself, but it was simply *a story* now, something that did what I always did with my novels. Take the real and alter it just enough, no matter how odd the real was, throw another wrench in the machinery, and describe what happened.

Maybe now I could move on.

Aftermath was released almost four years after Frank's suicide to much acclaim. Some called it my best novel. I ignored the reviews. It didn't really matter to me what anybody thought. After all, their opinions were shaped by a world in which I no longer found value.

My publisher had set up book signings and television appearances, blog interviews, podcasts, and every other form of internet intrusion.

I ignored these as well.

The novel took on a life of its own, became my best-selling book. I could care less. I sent it off much as a mother bird would kick a baby bird out of the nest to fly or flounder, not really caring whether it did or not.

I knew it was my best work. So what? All along as I wrote it, something nipped at the back of my neck. A thought that never left me, no matter my desire to move on from the experience.

I was different now. I'd had a taste of something profound and knew there was more to this life than book tours and meeting my public and even the process of writing. I knew there was more than what the human mind and human experiences could genuinely engage. I knew there was living to be had that was of a more fundamental foundation than the aspirations that clogged the heads of most people. The ideals that filled my head were no longer of this insipid ilk, yet trying to understand their rationale left me mentally exhausted.

As a fantasist my whole life, it saddened me that I lacked the appropriate imagination to envision the possibilities.

With this thought, I knew I had found my answer…

Standing in Frank's empty house for the first time in four years, I felt the presence hesitantly reacquainting itself with me. It knew me well enough to keep its distance; I knew to keep my head clear and strong as to the choice I had made by even being here again.

I'd already wandered through the house, sucked in the stale air devoid of life, though signs of stragglers and what-not were evident by make-shift beds—blankets, a couple of dust-coated pillows— and garbage—crumpled bags from Skunks, drained bottles of alcohol. Despite what Frank had done, graffiti filled the walls, love letters from fans unwilling to let him go.

I wondered what had happened to the stragglers, but really, it did not matter. Their fate was not of my concern.

My fate was.

As I leaned on the wood stove, "Bradford" firm beneath my palm, I breathed deeply and steadied myself. It wasn't as if I was afraid. I was ready to make the final move. Though this place was hesitant in feeling me out, hesitation was not a part of my repertoire at this point. I just needed to feel the air enter my lungs again, to fill myself to bursting, only to exhale with force.

I knew what I was doing. I knew what I had to do.

I stepped through the back door and stretched my arms, taking another deep breath, fresh air this time, cleansing my soul. I glanced toward Alethea's house, having gently knocked on her door when I had arrived, expecting nothing and nothing received, foolishly encouraged by the ephemeral time her fantasy doppelganger had participated in my life. A moment of weakness, fleeting as I marched with determination toward the forest.

(…*and a gentle sound nudges at my door, not really a knock, but with aspirations towards being one. I paused, pulling my focus from my eyes and the quartz crystal, to my ears, and the secrets these other sounds might wish to reveal to me. Nothing follows, and I shift again, back to the quartz crystal…)*

This place had shown me a side of Frank that I might never have seen. I hated being shown this at first, but over time, I have grown to understand what it really had done. It had shown me its soul, something unlimited, uninhibited. Sure, this place might have tendencies that leaned toward a kind of tarnished appreciation of evil, but it was not, as Frank had conjectured, essentially evil.

At least this is what I have convinced myself is true, because amidst the madness, there was beauty as well. Alethea was confirmation of that much.

Frank, in his resigned denouement, had always said of my writing there was hope. I understood that it wasn't hope I catered to, but a willingness to never allow the circumstances to hinder *the possibilities*. Much as Alethea had said. Alethea, a voice from within, a deeper part of *my* consciousness made concrete.

Though this place lacked a conscience or consciousness to call its own, it had the ability to change things, to create without limitations, and it had granted me a gift that most people would deem unwanted, without realizing the breadth of what the gift entailed: it had granted me a sort of freedom, a freedom that stood all fantasy on its head.

The freedom to simply be, nothing more.

I had once spent time as a tree, and, despite the finale, those few minutes or hours had been the most perfect hours of this existence. At least when Aleister had pulled his hand from me and let me simply be, nothing more.

I have cleared my head of anything negative and am ready to embrace that which was always mine.

I sense Alethea beyond my vision as I enter the forest, the smell of her, the vitality of her, but it is not a desire to see her that drives me onward. Maybe she will join me as one, though, a funny thought, since the Alethea that I knew is already a part of me. The real Alethea is probably hundreds of miles away, wrapped up in a recording session.

(…I see him. Through the quartz crystal, I see him: Derek Gray, the writer who had been present for the chaos that had transpired in the house

next to mine, and this forest. A man who has always fascinated me with his use of words, his handsome visage, his presence, no matter the fact that we have never met. I've seen interviews, read articles, and he always seemed like somebody who would make sense to me.

But this is different. This is not his face, this is the whole of him, and he is moving, walking. I wonder how this can be. I stare into the quartz crystal, mystified at this new revelation. Is this what the forest has decided to show me? Normally I see his face, a cracked mirror visage via the crystal—calcite crystal in my dreams; quartz crystal in my…day dreams? Wishes…? Yet with a melding of the pieces over time. Now, I see him in a way I've never seen him. Movement, as if he is here, as if—)

I make it to that barren glade and it is as I remember it. Vast and empty yet no images dance in the spider webs.

I take off my clothes, toss them to the ground.

My head is clear and strong to the task at hand. Giving up to the unseen forces around me, with the knowledge that something evil is not in the cards.

That's not who *I* am.

I stand naked and invite this place to show me once more the unconditional freedom I had experienced in its presence.

Have I ever really imagined? Has my life as a writer—no—*as a human being*, been nothing more than prelude to the true definition of life—*of being alive*—that I had experienced out here?

It is all too much…

It is all so perfect…it overwhelms, it enthralls…i am in awe…i am alive…*i am*…

Then—

—I realize, as the figure moves beyond the borders of the quartz crystal—as Derek Gray moves beyond the borders of the quartz crystal— past the now trembling fingers that hold the crystal, that the forest's intent has been made clear…

*I set the quartz crystal down next to a journal, where I have scribbled my thoughts about this man, this forest, and magic, and exit the back door of the house—*this *house, at the edge of* this *forest—and march with determination toward the forest, and the man who has filled my visions for so long, the man who has disappeared into the trees, thinking,* Please don't disappear…

I make it to a large tree amidst a barren glade and stop. A beautiful, majestic being, so full of character and warmth.

The sounds around me come alive. I hear with all of me, the sounds caressing me, my ears, my flesh, and my soul.

The leaves shimmer and whisper to me: "Alethea."

I embrace the tree, my unexpectedly naked flesh soothed by the rough hide. I say, "Yes," and await their response.

The response reverberates within me, a singular voice, a man's voice—Derek Gray's voice—saying my name: "Alethea." It is with the seeds of astonishment and the greatest of love that he speaks my name. His voice in my head, because he cannot speak any other way.

Because he is the tree.

I know this as I know my name, my heart and soul, the being I am, yet, what do I truly know of myself?

I say again, "Yes," nodding my head enthusiastically, with an understanding of what is about to happen. I invite this place to show me an unconditional freedom that I have never experienced.

It makes me question my life up to this point: Have I ever really imagined? Has my life as a musician—no—as a human being, been nothing more than prelude to the true definition of life—of being alive— that I hope to experience here?

It is all too much...yet I want to experience it all.

It is all so perfect...it overwhelms, it enthralls...i am in awe....i am alive...i am...

Then—

—the more perfect realization
—the more perfect realization

within this life comes to both of us:
within this life comes to both of us:

an understanding of possibilities…
an understanding of possibilities…

We exist in ways that expand the chains
we exist in ways that expand the chains

of confinement to a place of
of conf'nement to a place of

infinite inclusion of everything.
infinite inclusion of everything.

We are the earth.
We are the earth.

We are the sky…the air…
We are the sky…the air…

We are the reality that is
We are the reality that is

pure unconditional love.
pure unconditional love.

We are one.

 John Claude Smith has published two collections (*The Dark is Light Enough for Me* and *Autumn in the Abyss*), four chapbooks (*Dandelions, Vox Terrae, The Anti-Everything*, and *The Wrath of Concrete and Steel*), and one novel. The novel, *Riding the Centipede*, was published by Omnium Gatherum in 2015, and was a Bram Stoker Award finalist for Superior Achievement in a First Novel. He splits his time between the East Bay of northern California, across from San Francisco, and Rome, Italy, where his heart resides always.

CPSIA information can be obtained
at www.ICGtesting.com
Printed in the USA
LVOW11s1939011017
550729LV00002B/2/P